三版

全民英檢 聽力測驗

初級篇

SO EASY

三民英語編輯小組　彙整

最新穎！符合全新改版英檢題型
最逼真！模擬試題提升應試能力
最精闢！範例分析傾授高分技巧

 附 解答本 電子朗讀音檔

三民書局

新制全民英檢測驗是為了因應教育部 108 課綱，在測驗題型上做了些調整，以符合現代人對英文的需求。因此，我們分析了財團法人語言訓練測驗中心所公告之內容，將本書做了全新改版，為考生做全方位的準備。

不過，在繼續往下閱讀或甚至考慮購買之前，請先問自己是不是：

　　□ 需要通過全民英檢初級考試的人
　　□ 想要增進英文聽力的人
　　□ 對國際化趨勢有警覺的人
　　□ 習慣性涉獵各種主題書本的人

只要以上四個選項中，有任何一個符合你的情況，那麼，請繼續閱讀。因為時間是很寶貴的，本書將協助你節省時間，讓你事半功倍。

在開始進入書中的試題之前，我們先談一下國際化與全民英檢，因為這關係到為何參加全民英檢測驗，以及為什麼你正在閱讀本書。接著，要參加全民英檢測驗或對它有興趣的人應該知道全民英檢是什麼。最後針對本書的聽力練習，分享一些聽力的基本原則與技巧。

國際化與全民英檢

在談論全民英檢之前，讓我們先來看看國際化與全民英檢的關聯。不可否認地，英文已成為世界各國、各行各業，甚至是網路上溝通的主要語言。因此，在國際化的趨勢下，我們對英文有越來越多需求。全民英檢其實是這個趨勢下的產物。在英文如此重要的時代下，越來越多公司在招募人才時，會要求全民英檢的通過證明。另外，越來越多國內外學校在接受申請或甄試學生時，也將全民英檢的認證當作一個標準。教育部更逐年提高各級學校學生必須通過全民英檢的比例。

什麼是全民英檢？

全民英檢的全名是 General English Proficiency Test (GEPT)。所謂的 "proficiency test"，並不只是測驗聽、說、讀、寫任何單方面的能力，而是一個人能使用該語言溝通的能力。因此 "English proficiency test" 就是一個人能使用英文溝通，並且表達自我的能力。所以，全民英檢是沒有範圍的，並非讀完固定的十本或五十本書就必定會拿滿分的一種測驗。全民英檢的目的在於：測驗一個人是否能用英文在聽、說、讀、寫於各種不同的環境下，適當的表達自己並了解別人。其成績也能對照 CEFR（國際認證的英語程度指標）。

以下將為你介紹全民英檢的三大特色：

1. 分級測驗

全民英檢分成五個級數：初級、中級、中高級、高級及優級。初級程度應具備基礎的英文能力，能夠理解並運用簡單的日常用語；中級程度應在日常生活中，能使用簡易的英文溝通；中高級程度應具備較成熟的英文能力，可能不是很精確的用語，但能在生活上溝通無礙；高級程度應具備流利的英文能力，少有錯誤並能於專業領域中運用；優級程度則應具備接近已受高等教育英語母語人士的英文能力，能在各場合做專業有效的溝通。

2. 聽、說、讀、寫四技並重

既然全民英檢是測驗一個人使用英文溝通與生存的能力，當然考試就不應只重視四技中的任何一技。因此，全民英檢有聽讀測驗和說寫測驗，其中口說與寫作測驗可以單項報名。建議通過聽讀測驗後，再報名說寫測驗，因為口語表達與寫作能力這兩項產出能力，遠比能聽讀這兩項接收能力來得困難。

3. 日常生活化的題型

同樣的，要測試一個人溝通的能力，當然題型就該反映這樣的測驗目的。因此，大部份試題的情境是與日常生活相關的，如問路、點餐等。而運用的詞彙也和生活息息相關。若試題中出現了臺灣並不常見的字詞，如 macaroni 與 artichokes 等西方常見的食物與蔬菜，考生可能會因為生活經驗不足，而非語文能力不足而無法作答。因此，試題中會出現夜市、火車站、米、醬油等常用字彙，讓考生在測驗時，能在熟悉的場景中，專注於語言相關的部份。

初級聽力的基本原則與技巧

在學習任何一個語言時，最自然的程序是聽、說、讀，最後是寫。因此聽力是語言學習的根本。當然，母語與非母語無論在學習過程或環境上來說，都大不相同，但學習目的卻永遠一致，那就是溝通。我們聽懂語言也是為了溝通，因為溝通成功，我們就能了解對方與所在環境，進而做出適當的回應。因為聽的目的是溝通，我們應該學會聽懂重點。若能成功抓到重點，即便無法聽懂每一個字，溝通仍然可以繼續；但若無法抓到重點，溝通則立即失敗。

全民英檢初級聽力分為四個部份：看圖辨義、問答、簡短對話及短文聽解。這四個部份基本上都遵循溝通與切中要點的原則與技巧。所以,看圖辨義的部份,應該看的是整張圖所要表達的意思。同樣地,當你聽簡短對話時,應該注意說話者可能的所在位置、二人關係等對話重點,而不是第三人稱是否有加 s 這樣的細節。至於問答的部份,通常第一個字很重要,因為問題通常是以 Who、Where、What、How 等字開始。若能抓到第一個字,就有極高的機率能答對。不過,也要仔細聽問題的內容,才能選出對應且適當的回答。短文聽解的部份,則是要聽懂題目在問什麼,除了抓住疑問詞之外,還要清楚圖片所傳遞的訊息,再仔細聆聽短文中的內容,才能選出正確的答案。更詳細的說明,請至全民英檢網站查閱,讓自己更認識即將接觸的測驗。

本書初版由三民英語編輯小組彙整,車畇庭教授審訂,三版則由三民英語編輯小組以前版為基礎調整內容,全新改版。相信你已經準備好了,那麼現在就請你繼續閱讀,進一步了解全民英檢初級聽力測驗的每一部份該如何準備,然後開始進行實戰練習吧!

電子朗讀音檔下載

請先輸入網址或掃描 QR code 進入「三民‧東大音檔網」
https://elearning.sanmin.com.tw/Voice/

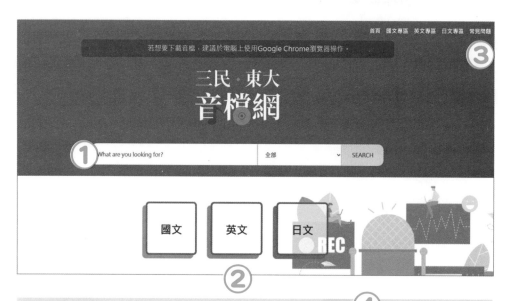

三民東大 外文組- 英文	若有音檔相關問題，歡迎**聯絡我們** ④ 服務時間：週一-週五，08:00-17:30 臉書粉絲專頁：**Sanmin English - 三民英語編輯小組** ⑤

① 輸入本書書名即可找到音檔。請再依提示下載音檔。

② 也可點擊「英文」進入英文專區查找音檔後下載。

③ 若無法順利下載音檔，可至「常見問題」查看相關問題。

④ 若有音檔相關問題，請點擊「聯絡我們」，將盡快為你處理。

⑤ 更多英文新知都在臉書粉絲專頁。

全民英檢聽力測驗
SO EASY （初級篇）

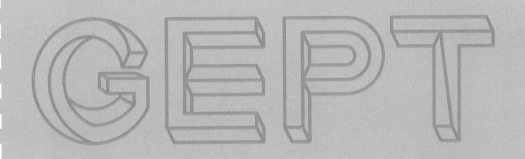

聽力測驗試題範例分析

第一部份：看圖辨義

此部份的聽力題目圍繞在一張情境圖上，圖裡具備一定程度的線索，讓答題者觀察並聆聽問題與選項。請特別注意：問題與選項都是完全以聽力的方式呈現，不會有文字在試卷上。

依圖片的情境與題目所詢問的內容，我們先將這部份題目分為主旨題（Main Idea）、細節題（Details）、推論題（Inference）等三種類型；並且依題目線索 What、Where、When、Who、Why、How、How + adj. 等不同的疑問詞，去思考答題方向。

以下我們就以五個範例來介紹各種題型與答題技巧吧！

A. Question 1

For question number 1, please look at picture A.

Question number 1: How does the boy like the fish?

(A) He is having his lunch.

(B) He doesn't like it very much.

(C) It's his favorite dish.

翻 譯

第一題，請看圖片 A。

第一題：這男孩覺得這盤魚如何？

選項：(A) 他正在吃午餐。

(B) 他很不喜歡這盤魚。

(C) 那是他最愛的菜餚。

解 析

本題為主旨題 (Main Idea)，也就是這張圖片最想呈現的意思。當一眼看到這張圖片時，最容易注意到的事情、人物或表情等。以此題為例，這個男孩的表情明顯告訴我們他不喜歡。因此，不管這道菜是魚、肉或蛋糕，其實都不是重點，重點是「這個男孩不喜歡」。在聽到題目問 How 時，就應知道題目主要問的是喜好、感覺的部份，再對照男孩的表情，答案呼之欲出。

答 案　　B

B. Question 2

For question number 2, please look at picture B.

Question number 2: Where are they?

(A) They are in a meeting room.

(B) They are in a kitchen.

(C) They are at a bus station.

翻 譯

第二題,請看圖片 B。

第二題:他們在什麼地方?

選項:(A) 他們在會議室裡。

　　　(B) 他們在廚房裡。

　　　(C) 他們在公車站。

解 析

這張圖片的構圖較為複雜,以一般所熟悉的狀況來看,應該是中間位置這個男人為會議主持者,總共有七人參加。這種較不容易直接獲得答題訊息的題目,極有可能就是推論題 (Inference)。整個場景與他們的穿著,很容易判定這可能是在會議室或辦公室。因此,當聽到題目的第一個字是 Where 時,就可以直接等待答案 "meeting room" 或 "office" 的出現。

答 案　　**A**

C. Questions 3 and 4

For questions number 3 and 4, please look at picture C.

Question number 3: Who is the man?

(A) He is a clerk.

(B) He has just bought a drink.

(C) He likes playing computer games.

翻譯

第三題及第四題，請看圖片 C。

第三題：這男生是誰？

選項：(A) 他是一位店員。

(B) 他剛買了一罐飲料。

(C) 他喜歡玩電腦遊戲。

解析

接下來的第三題及第四題是從一張圖片考兩個問題。這張圖片從整體來看，可以馬上判定這個場景是一家商店，女孩正拿著鈔票準備結帳。這種畫面有較多線索，就要想到可能為主旨題 *(Main Idea)*、細節題 *(Details)* 或甚至是推論題 *(Inference)*，完全依疑問詞來判定。在聽到 *Who* 加上 "man" 時，就可以馬上想到答案了。另外，同樣的圖片也可能會用 What 問「他們在做什麼」、「女孩買了什麼」、「女孩付的是什麼」、「男生操作的是什麼機器」或用 Where 問「他們在哪裡」等。

答案   **A**

Question number 4, please look at picture C again.

What is the man most likely saying to the woman?

(A) Keep the change.

(B) How much do these cost?

(C) The total is 100 dollars.

翻譯

第四題，請再看一次圖片 C。

這男生最有可能對這女生說什麼？

選項：(A) 不用找零了。

(B) 這些多少錢？

(C) 總共一百元。

解析

另外，有人物的圖片題，除了觀察人物正在進行的動作，也要注意情境。這題的人物為一位店員與一位顧客，聽到 most likely 就可以知道是推論題 (Inference)，要推論可能發生的事。聽到這題的關鍵字 What、"man" 和 "saying" 就能知道考的是男生說了什麼話。圖中可知男生是店員，因此能進而推論他可能說的話。而這類題目可能用 What 問「可能在說什麼」、用 Where 問「說話者可能在哪裡」、用 Who 問「說話者可能是什麼關係」、「說話者可能是誰」等的問題。因此，答題技巧就是要仔細聽疑問詞是什麼、是問 "man" 還是 "woman"，並觀察圖片中人物的動作來思考可能的答案。

答案 C

D. Question 5

Lily's School Schedule

(Monday)

9:00	Chinese
10:00	English
11:00	English
12:00	Lunch
13:30	Math
14:30	History
15:30	Swimming

For question number 5, please look at picture D.

Question number 5: How many hours of English does Lily have on Monday?

(A) One hour.

(B) One and half hours.

(C) Two hours.

翻譯

第五題,請看圖片 D。

第五題:莉莉星期一有幾個小時的英文課?

選項:(A) 一個小時。

(B) 一個半小時。

(C) 兩個小時。

解析

這張圖片是典型的細節題 (Details),當然,也有可能以 What 問「這是什麼」這樣的問題,不過可能比較少見。基本上來說,題目會與日程表中的時間或需要做的事情相關。因此,當聽到 How many hours (*How + adj.* 類型),加上 "English" 時,就可以直接找答案了。

答案   C

聽力測驗試題範例分析

第二部份：問答

此部份的聽力題目僅僅只有一句話，答題者必須做的，是根據聽到的這句話，在試卷上列出的三個選項中，找出一個最適當的回應。由於答題選項會呈現在試卷上，不會因為聽力播放過之後就消失，因此事先觀察選項內容和判斷問題的屬性就成了最重要的技巧。

首先，我們可以將這部份的題目分為三種：直述句、Wh- 問句、非 Wh- 問句；並且針對該句話的情境，去思考適當的回應，然後選出正確的選項。我們歸類出最常見的情境有下列幾種：打招呼 (Greeting)、請求 (Request)、詢問 (Inquiry)、建議 (Suggestion)、表達感謝 (Gratitude)、致歉 (Apology)、稱讚 (Compliment)、陳述 (Statement)。

以下我們就以十個範例來介紹各種題型與答題技巧吧！

1 Let's go to the movies tonight.

  (A) I'm sorry, but I have a test tomorrow.

  (B) I was very happy that day.

  (C) No, thanks. I'm quite full.

翻　譯

我們今晚去看電影吧。

選項：(A) 很抱歉，我明天有個考試。

  (B) 那天我很高興。

  (C) 不，謝了。我吃得很飽。

提　示

→ 題目的型態是**直述句**。

→ 題目的涵義是**建議**，向對方提議今晚要不要去看電影。

解　析

這題可先判斷出是一個直述句，而非疑問句。"Let" 開頭的句子有很明顯的涵義，就是「提議」、「建議」的意思。要回應這樣的句子有幾種可能：

(1) 接受對方的建議（後面可能會接一些贊同的詞彙）。

(2) 拒絕對方的建議（後面可能會敘述拒絕的理由或原因）。

本題的選項 (A) 就是第 (2) 種情形，先表示抱歉，然後說出理由。選項 (B) 的回答和題目沒有關聯，而選項 (C) 雖然表達了拒絕之意，但後面的理由與題目完全不相關，所以都不是正確答案。

答　案　**A**

2 How are you?

  (A) Nice to meet you, too.

  (B) Fine. How about you?

  (C) The weather is fine.

翻　譯

你好嗎？

選項：(A) 我也很高興認識你。

　　　(B) 很好，你呢？

　　　(C) 今天天氣不錯。

提 示

→ 題目的型態是 **Wh- 問句**。

→ 題目的涵義是**打招呼**，常見於雙方見面的時候。

解 析

這題的題目是 "How" 開頭的 Wh- 問句，通常是問感覺或對人、事、物的喜好或厭惡程度。例如這一句問的就是「你好嗎？」，是一個典型的問候語，因此在回答問題時，要告知對方的是好或不好，或問候對方，才算是一個得體的對應。當然，在一個典型的問候與回答社交用語中，通常不會告知對方自己過得不好，而會十分制式地表示很好，因此選項 (B) 為正確答案。本題答案中，選項 (A) 應為對方說 "Nice to meet you." 時的回答語，而選項 (C) 則是一個不相干的回應，利用句中的 "fine" 作為誘答的字彙。

答 案　　**B**

3　　Could you open the window for me?

　　　(A) Yes, please.

　　　(B) Sure. Right away.

　　　(C) Not at all.

翻 譯

你能幫我把窗戶打開嗎？

選項：(A) 是的，請。

　　　(B) 當然。我馬上幫你開。

　　　(C) 不客氣。

→ 題目的型態是**非 *Wh-* 問句**。

→ 題目的涵義是**請求**，請對方幫忙把窗戶打開。

解 析

這題的第一個字是 "Could"，一聽到這個字，應該馬上聯想到答案是與肯定或否定相關，因為這類的問句通常是「詢問可不可以做某事」或「請求其他人做某事」，本題即為後者。因此，這類的題目通常牽涉的是 yes 或 no 的答案。不過以這一題的答案來看，選項 (A) 是一個誘答的錯誤選項，選項 (B) 反而才是正確答案。大部份的人在聽到 could，然後聯想到 yes 或 no 的答案時，一看到選項 (A) 中的 "Yes" 往往就會以為是正確答案，但這時還是要務必小心將整個選項看完才作答。以這裡的 "Yes, please." 為例，意思就完全顛倒了，因為這是在對方詢問自己某事之後，自己同意才這樣回答，例如："Would you like to have some tea?" "Yes, please."。而選項 (B) 雖然沒有用 "yes"，但是 "sure" 這個字有類似的肯定涵義，因此符合此問句的回答。而選項 (C) 則是謝謝的回覆用語，與本題毫無關聯。

答 案　　**B**

4　　Can I see Mr. Wang this morning?

(A) I will see Mr. Wang later.

(B) Yes, this morning is beautiful.

(C) Sorry. He is very busy.

翻 譯

我能在今天早上見王先生嗎？

選項：(A) 等一下我會見到他。

　　　(B) 是的，今天早上很漂亮。

　　　(C) 抱歉。他非常忙碌。

提 示

→ 題目的型態是**非 *Wh-* 問句**。

→ 題目的涵義是**詢問**，提出見面的要求請對方回答。

這一題的第一個字是 "Can"，與上一題都是屬於同類型的題目，只是 could 較常用於請求，而 can 多用於詢問可不可以。一般而言，could 比較禮貌、客氣，但大部份的情況下，兩者是可以互換的。這題問的是「能不能見王先生」，因此回答應該是可以或有困難而不行。選項 (A) 與 (B) 都是誘答選項，因為這兩個答案中都刻意用了題目中出現的字，選項 (B) 更以 "Yes" 開頭，但都不適當。而本題的正確選項 (C) 雖然沒有直接用 yes 或 no，但與上一題一樣用了替代的字（上一題是 sure 表示肯定，而這一題是 sorry 表示否定），間接地表示不能見王先生。

答 案　　**C**

5　Thank you for such a wonderful dinner.

(A) I'm glad you liked it.

(B) Yes, it's too much.

(C) Oh, come on! It's too late to go now.

翻 譯

謝謝你招待我這麼棒的晚餐。

選項：(A) 很高興你喜歡。

　　　(B) 是的，的確是太過頭了。

　　　(C) 噢，別這樣！現在已經太晚，不能離開了。

提 示

→ 題目的型態是**直述句**。

→ 題目的涵義是**表達感謝**，表示出自己的心境。

解 析

在第二部份的問答中，直述句與針對這個敘述所做的回應也是很重要的一種類型。這題的直述句是典型表示感謝的句子，因為句子的開始就是 "Thank you for . . . ."，除了感謝好吃的晚餐之外，還可以感謝下午茶 (afternoon tea)、一段快樂的時光 (wonderful time)、好看的電影 (movie)、很棒的禮物 (gift)，或任何值得感謝的事情。回應表達感謝的句子可以是："You are most welcome."、"Glad you liked it."、

"Not at all."、"My pleasure." 等等。本題的選項 (A) 就是典型的回應；而選項 (B) 則完全不恰當，因為在對方表達謝意之後，我們不該有這種反應；至於選項 (C) 的前半段雖然可以適用於好友之間的對話，但後半段則完全離題，因此這個回應為誘答選項。

6　The cake you made was very delicious.

    (A) Yes, please.

    (B) Have a nice day.

    (C) Oh, thank you!

翻 譯

你做的蛋糕非常美味。

選項：(A) 好，麻煩你了。

      (B) 祝你有美好的一天。

      (C) 噢，謝謝！

提 示

→ 題目的型態是直述句。

→ 題目的涵義是稱讚，表達出對其他人、事、物的肯定。

解 析

這個題目與上一題同樣是直述句，只不過上一題是表示感謝，而這題則是稱讚。在聽到 "cake" 與 "delicious" 之後，馬上能聯想到 "Thank you very much."、"Glad you liked it." 等回應。本題的選項 (C) 就是一個非常普遍又簡單的回應。選項 (A) 適用於 "Would you like to have a piece of cake?" 這樣的問句；而選項 (B) 則是道別的用語，與本題完全不相關。

答 案　C

7　I think we are lost.

(A) You should rest there.

(B) Maybe we should ask someone else.

(C) I don't have money, either.

翻譯

我想我們迷路了。

選項：(A) 你應該在那邊休息。

(B) 也許我們應該問問別人。

(C) 我也沒有錢。

提示

→ 題目的型態是直述句。

→ 題目的涵義是陳述，用來敘述事實或自己的想法。

解析

這題仍然是個直述句，但是屬於陳述事情的狀況，比較不帶有太多的情感成分。不過事實上，這句話隱含徵詢意見的意思，也就是希望回應的人能給一個建議。選項 (A) 是一個建議，但情境與迷路不符；而選項 (C) 則是 "I don't have money." 的回應，與迷路同樣是沒有關聯的；只有選項 (B) 的句子是針對迷路所提的建議。

答案 B

8 I bought this camera here yesterday. Could you take a look at it?

(A) I'll pay you money.

(B) I'm sorry. We're not on sale.

(C) What's the problem?

翻譯

我昨天在這裡買了這臺相機。你可以檢查一下嗎？

選項：(A) 我會付你錢。

(B) 很抱歉。我們現在沒有特賣活動。

(C) 是什麼問題呢？

→ 題目的型態是非 *Wh-* 問句。

→ 題目的涵義是請求,請對方幫忙檢視一下昨天剛買的相機。

解 析

這題的句子分成兩個部份,第一部份,也就是第一個句子,其實是第二部份的背景敘述,第二部份才是真正的問題。第一部份的關鍵字為 "bought"、"here" 和 "yesterday",一聽到這三個字,就應該要去設想說話者「在某個地方買了某樣東西」。接著,再聽到第二部份的第一個字為 "Could" 時,就可以猜想買的這個東西可能出了問題,因此要店家幫忙檢查 (take a look at it/check it)/換貨 (exchange)/退費 (refund) 等。也因此,最可能的回應應該會是 "What's the problem?" 或是 "What's wrong?" 之類的句子。本題的選項 (A) 有誘答性,但比較像是買方對賣方所說的話,而不是賣方對買方說的話;選項 (B) 雖然是店員會說的話,但與先前問的事情不相關;只有選項 (C) 是針對題目的背景敘述與狀況所做出的回應。

答 案　　**C**

9　　What color do you prefer?

(A) I like black.

(B) Yes, red is better than blue.

(C) Do you have other size?

翻 譯

你比較喜歡什麼顏色?

選項:(A) 我喜歡黑色。

　　　(B) 是的,紅色比藍色好。

　　　(C) 你們有別的尺寸嗎?

提 示

→ 題目的型態是 *Wh-* 問句。

→ 題目的涵義是詢問,內容是對於顏色的喜好。

解析

這題的關鍵字是 "What" 和 "color"，如果有聽到這兩個字，就可以了解這題想問的是顏色，而且應該不需要回答 "yes" 或 "no"。選項 (C) 提到尺寸大小，所以可以馬上判定這一定是錯的。至於另外兩個選項，選項 (B) 以 "Yes" 開頭，雖有提到顏色，但並不是針對這個問句所做的回應，它應該是 "Do you think red is better than blue?" 的回答。選項 (A) 直接說明喜歡的顏色，因此是此題的正確答案。

答案　**A**

10　I'd like to make a reservation for 5 people for tonight.

　　　(A) Sure. Your name, please.

　　　(B) Today's special is fish and chips.

　　　(C) Tomorrow will be fine.

翻譯

我想預訂今天晚上五個人的位子。

選項：(A) 沒問題。請告訴我您的大名。

　　　(B) 今天的特餐是炸魚薯條。

　　　(C) 明天的話沒問題。

提示

→ 題目的型態是直述句。

→ 題目的涵義是請求，跟店家（可推論是餐廳）預約訂位。

解析

這題是一個請求的直述句，關鍵字為 "make a reservation"，告訴對方要訂位。以常理來判斷，最有可能做出 "Sure, what time would you like it to be?"、"What is your name, please?" 等與訂位相關的回應。三個選項中只有選項 (A) 是與訂位相關；而選項 (B) 雖與餐廳與食物相關，但應該是 "What is today's special?"（本日特餐是什麼？）的回應；至於選項 (C) 則與本題無關。

答案　**A**

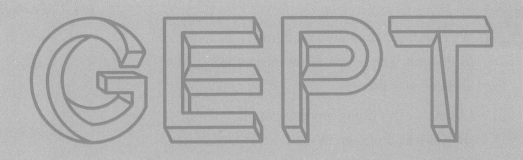

聽力測驗試題範例分析

第三部份：簡短對話

此部份的聽力題目是一段簡短的兩人對話，然後再從一個中立的角度，問一個問題。答題者必須做的，是根據聽到的這個問題，在列在試卷上的三個選項中，找出一個最適當的答案。雖然答題選項是直接呈現在試卷上，但由於題目內容較長且複雜，要很快判斷選項的狀況並不容易，因此還是要回歸到最基本的立足點，就是把題目聽懂。

與第一部份的分類方法相同，我們先依對話的情境與所詢問的內容，將其分為主旨題 (Main Idea)、細節題 (Details)、推論題 (Inference) 等；然後針對問法跟疑問詞的不同（Yes/No 問句、Wh- 問句等），去思考選項中的正確答案。

以下我們就以十個範例來介紹各種題型與答題技巧吧！

1 W: Hi, Dave. How are you doing?

M: Couldn't be better. How about you?

Q: How was Dave?

(A) He wasn't doing anything at all.

(B) He was doing great.

(C) He has nothing special.

翻 譯

女：嗨，戴夫。你好嗎？

男：再好不過了。你呢？

問題：戴夫過得如何？

選項：(A) 他什麼事也沒做。

(B) 他過得很好。

(C) 他沒什麼特別之處。

提 示

→ 本題屬於細節題 (Details)。

→ 題目的疑問詞是 How，用來詢問感覺、狀況。

解 析

這段簡短對話是一般見面時的問候與回覆語，"How are you doing?" 相當於 "How do you do?" 或 "How are you?" 或 "What's up?"。不管是哪一種問法，都可以用 "Couldn't be better."（再好不過了。）來回答。這一句話在生活中經常被用來形容一個人對自己或某件事的感覺，例如這個人對自身的感覺或正在進行中的計畫進度等等。本題的疑問詞是 How，以它開頭的問句通常問的就是感覺或狀況。這題問的是戴夫的狀況，而選項 (B) 中的 "doing great" 就是指某人很好，與做什麼事情完全無關。至於選項 (A) 與 (C) 則應該是針對 What 開頭的問句所給的回應。

答 案 B

2 M: Hi, Ms. Chen. May I speak to Jenny, please?

W: May I ask who's calling?

M: This is Tom, Jenny's classmate.

W: Hold on a second.

Q: What are they doing?

(A) They are speaking to Jenny.

(B) They are talking on the phone.

(C) They are waiting for someone.

翻譯

男：嗨，陳小姐。麻煩你，我可以請珍妮聽電話嗎？

女：請問是哪位？

男：我是湯姆，珍妮的同學。

女：請等一下。

問題：他們在做什麼？

選項：(A) 他們正在跟珍妮講話。

(B) 他們正在講電話。

(C) 他們正在等某人。

提示

→ 本題屬於主旨題 (Main Idea)。

→ 題目的疑問詞是 What，用來詢問「什麼」。

解析

這題問的是 "What are they doing?"。在一段對話之後問這樣的問題，我們可以馬上判定問的是對話主旨，也就是要由整段對話內容去判斷答案，而不是其中任何單一的細節。這段對話中有不少十分典型的句子，例如 "May I speak to . . . ?"、"Who's calling?"、"Hold on a second."，只要一聽到這幾句，幾乎可以馬上判定這二個人在講電話，所以本題答案非常明顯為選項 (B)。至於選項 (A) 與 (C) 則是誘答選項，選項 (A) 中出現了 "Jenny"，是在對話中出現的人名；而選項 (C) 中則針對 "hold" 而捏造出 "waiting for" 這樣的內容。

答案　　**B**

3 W: Can I borrow your bicycle during lunchtime?

M: I'm sorry. I have to use it this noon.

Q: Can the woman borrow the man's bicycle?

(A) Yes. She can use it.

(B) No. He will use it.

(C) No. He doesn't have any bicycle.

翻 譯

女：午餐時間我可以跟你借腳踏車嗎？

男：很抱歉。今天中午我要用車。

問題：這女生能借到這男生的腳踏車嗎？

選項：(A) 是的。她可以使用它。

(B) 不。他將要用到它。

(C) 不。他並沒有腳踏車。

提 示

→ 本題屬於主旨題 *(Main Idea)*。

→ 題目的問法是 *Yes/No* 問句，通常要回答 "yes" 或 "no"。

解 析

這題問句的第一個字是 Can，凡是此字開頭的問句，問的都是可不可以或能不能，因此答案通常是以 "yes" 或 "no" 開頭。在聽到 "I'm sorry." 這一句時，應該可以馬上將選項 (A) 剔除在外，因為那是委婉的拒絕回覆語。剩下的選項 (B) 與 (C) 則必須要稍微判斷一下，如果男子的回答是 "I don't have one." 或 "I don't ride a bike." 之類的句子，那麼選項 (C) 就是正確答案。不過這名男子用了 "use" 這個字，表示他有腳踏車而且他要使用，所以這題答案十分明顯是選項 (B)。

答 案　**B**

4 M: The steaks here are very good. Would you like to order one?

W: Gee, I'm sorry. I don't eat beef. Can I have fish?

Q: What are they talking about?

(A) Schoolwork.

(B) Outdoor activities.

(C) Food.

翻譯

男：這裡的牛排非常好吃。你想要點一客嗎？

女：啊，很抱歉。我不吃牛肉。我可以點魚嗎？

問題：他們正在談論什麼？

選項：(A) 學校功課。

　　　(B) 戶外活動。

　　　(C) 食物。

提示

→ 本題屬於主旨題 *(Main Idea)*。

→ 題目的疑問詞是 *What*，用來詢問「什麼」。

解析

這題的問題是他們在談論什麼，所以是一個非常典型問對話主旨的問題。在對話中出現了 "steaks"、"order"、"beef"、"fish" 這幾個與食物有關的字，把這些字串連在一起時，我們可以馬上斷定這個對話的場景是餐廳或賣食物的地方，而且這兩個人在點餐或討論食物。因此，這題的答案非常明顯是選項 (C)，選項 (A) 與 (B) 皆為與對話無關之選項。

答案　C

5

W: Hi, Mike. Are you doing anything on Saturday?

M: What's up?

W: I'm going to have a party at my apartment. Would you like to come?

M: Sure. What time?

W: Anytime after 7:00 p.m.

M: OK. I'll be there.

Q: What is Mike going to do on Saturday?

(A) He's going to a party.

(B) He's going to move to his new apartment.

(C) He will be home at 7:00 p.m.

翻 譯

女：嗨，麥克。你星期六有什麼計畫嗎？

男：有什麼事？

女：我將要在我的公寓裡辦一個派對。你願意來嗎？

男：好啊。什麼時候？

女：晚上七點以後都行。

男：沒問題。我一定到。

問題：星期六麥克將要做什麼？

選項：(A) 他將要去參加派對。

　　　(B) 他將要搬到他的新公寓去。

　　　(C) 他晚上七點會到家。

提 示

→ 本題屬於細節題 *(Details)*。

→ 題目的疑問詞是 *What*，用來詢問「什麼」。

解 析

這一段對話比前面幾題來得都要長，而且對話中有較多派對相關的訊息，因此很可能會考其中的細節，像是什麼事件、時間、地點等。當我們聽到 "What is . . . going to do?" 這樣的問題時，應該很清楚知道問的是對話提及的其中一個細節，所以答案十分明顯是選項 (A)。至於選項 (B) 與 (C) 則是典型的誘答選項，在裡面分別出現了對話中所提的時間 (7:00 p.m.) 和地點 (apartment)。答題者很有可能會因為聽到這兩個細節而誤判答案。

答 案　**A**

6　W: Quick, my son is having a high fever. I need help!

　　　M: OK, calm down. Give him to me and please wait outside.

W: No, I have to be with him. I am his mother!

M: Sorry, you can't be here when the doctor examines him.

Q: Where are the two people?

(A) In the police station.

(B) At the bus stop.

(C) In the hospital.

翻 譯

女：快，我兒子正在發高燒。我需要幫忙！

男：好，請冷靜點。把他交給我，然後請在外面稍等。

女：不行，我必須陪著他。我是他的母親啊！

男：抱歉，當醫生診治他的時候，你不能待在這裡。

問題：這兩人在什麼地方？

選項：(A) 在警察局裡。

(B) 在公車站。

(C) 在醫院裡。

提 示

→ 本題屬於推論題 *(Inference)*。

→ 題目的疑問詞是 *Where*，用來詢問「在什麼地方」。

解 析

這題問句以 Where 開頭，因此答案應該是地點，但是我們看到三個選項都是地點，所以並無法從其中的關聯性直接去判斷。也就是說，我們必須從對話的本身去類推尋找線索。這題的對話內容是小孩發高燒，媽媽很緊張地帶著他去看病，當我們聽到 "high fever"、"doctor"、"examines" 這三個字時，應該可以馬上判定對話的場景是醫院，而說話者的關係則是病人家屬與醫護人員。由於這題問的並非對話者的關係，而是對話的場景，所以答案應該是選項 (C)，選項 (A) 與 (B) 則與對話內容無關。

答 案　C

7

W: Susan is moving back to live with her parents.

M: That's because her father is sick, and she is the only child in the family.

Q: How many children are there in Susan's family?

(A) Zero.

(B) One.

(C) Three.

翻 譯

女：蘇珊將要搬回去跟她父母一起住。

男：那是因為她父親生病了，而她又是家裡唯一的孩子。

問題：蘇珊的家庭有幾個小孩？

選項：(A) 零個。

(B) 一個。

(C) 三個。

提 示

→ 本題屬於推論題 (Inference)。

→ 題目的疑問詞是 How + adj.，用來詢問程度或數量。

解 析

這題問的是 How many，也就是數量。如同上一題一樣，這題的三個選項都是數字，且與題目所問的有直接關聯，因此不可能在第一時間先剔除任何一個。我們一樣必須從對話的本身去尋找線索。這題的關鍵字為 "only child"，既然蘇珊是家中唯一的小孩，那麼本題的答案就是選項 (B)。要小心的是，這樣類似的題目變化不少，只要將對話中 "... and she is the only child in the family" 改成 "... and her two elder sisters are living in France"，這題的答案就會變成選項 (C)，或是將問題改成 "How many brothers and sisters does Susan have?"，答案將會是選項 (A)。

答 案　　B

8

M: I'm sorry I'm late.

W: What happened?

M: The train was almost an hour late. It wasn't really my fault.

Q: What is the man doing?

(A) He is making a mistake.

(B) He is taking the train.

(C) He is apologizing.

翻 譯

男：很抱歉我遲到了。

女：發生什麼事？

男：火車幾乎晚了一個小時。那真的不是我的錯。

問題：這男生在做什麼？

選項：(A) 他正在犯錯。

　　　(B) 他正在搭火車。

　　　(C) 他正在道歉。

提 示

→ 本題屬於**推論題** *(Inference)*。

→ 題目的疑問詞是 *What*，用來詢問「什麼」。

解 析

這段簡短對話討論的主題是一個男生正在解釋為何遲到。我們知道當一個人努力解釋自己所犯的過錯時，通常是在道歉，所以當這一題問這名男子在做什麼時，我們就可以推測他在試圖道歉。尤其這個對話的第一句就是 "I'm sorry . . . ."，讓選項 (C) 更明顯成為本題的答案。至於另外二個則是誘答選項，其中選項 (B) 與對話中所提到的火車有關，而選項 (A) 則是利用了 "mistake" 這個字與 "fault" 的相似意義來試圖混淆答題者。

答 案　　C

9

M: So, what do you think about this movie?

W: Oh, the story is bad, the cast is terrible, and the music is even worse.

M: Same here. I almost fell asleep quite a few times.

Q: How does the man like the movie?

(A) He likes it very much.

(B) He doesn't like it at all.

(C) He has never seen it.

翻譯

男：嗯，你覺得這部電影怎麼樣？

女：噢，故事很爛，演員很糟，音樂更是差到不行。

男：我同意。有好幾次我幾乎都快睡著了。

問題：這男生覺得這部電影怎麼樣？

選項：(A) 他非常喜歡這部電影。

(B) 他一點也不喜歡這部電影。

(C) 他從沒看過這部電影。

提示

→ 本題屬於推論題 (Inference)。

→ 題目的疑問詞是 How，用來詢問感覺、狀況。

解析

這段對話討論的是一部很糟的電影，從女生說 "bad"、"terrible"、"worse" 這幾個字我們可以知道，她並不喜歡這部電影，但男生並沒有直接表示。這時，聽懂 "Same here." 這句話就成了答題的關鍵，這表示男生的看法「跟女生是一樣的」。因此，這題答案就會是選項 (B)。選項 (A) 與 (B) 是相對立的選項，當然不可能成立；選項 (C) 沒有直接回答問題，同時根據前面的對話，也不可能成立。

答案　　**B**

10

W: We have a new student today. This is Jason Wang. Jason, why don't you introduce yourself to the class?

M: Hi, everyone. My name is Jason Wang, and I'm from Kaohsiung.

Q: Where are the speakers?

(A) In a classroom.

(B) In a library.

(C) On a school bus.

翻 譯

女：我們今天有一個新同學。這位是王傑森。傑森，何不跟全班同學自我介紹一下？

男：嗨，大家好。我的名字叫做王傑森，我來自高雄。

問題：這些說話者在什麼地方？

選項：(A) 在教室裡。

(B) 在圖書館裡。

(C) 在校車上。

提 示

→ 本題屬於推論題 *(Inference)*。

→ 題目的疑問詞是 *Where*，用來詢問「在什麼地方」。

解 析

這題問的是對話的地點，從關鍵字 "class"、"new student"、"introduce" 我們就幾乎可以判斷這個對話的場景是在學校，或更精確來說是在教室裡面，一位老師請新同學做自我介紹。在圖書館中通常不會發生這種情境，在校車上也不會，因此這題雖然三個選項都是地點，但其實非常容易作答。

答 案　　**A**

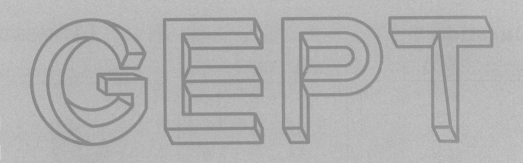

聽力測驗試題範例分析

第四部份：短文聽解

　　此部份的聽力題目為一段短文，內容包括廣播、留言等常見的日常生活情境。答題者必須依據短文的內容，從三個圖片中選出最適當的選項。短文內容皆以聽力的方式呈現，在試卷上不會有文字敘述。

　　值得注意的是，這個題型的聽力內容雖然較長，但不像第三部份是一來一往的簡短對話、談話內容複雜、要留意的訊息很多。本部份的聽力內容只是單一的敘述某一種情境，所以只要仔細聽並理解內容，就能一一的做出判斷，選出正確答案。

　　首先，在題目開始播放前，可以先留意一下三張圖片的情境。音檔一開始會先說明這是一則廣播、留言或是簡短談話等，接著會播出問題。聽完內容後，再根據問題與內容的關鍵字來找出適合的圖片作答。

　　以下我們就以五個範例來介紹各種題型與答題技巧吧！

Question 1

(A)　　　　　　　　　(B)　　　　　　　　　(C)

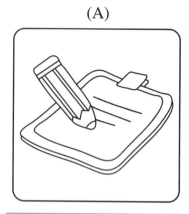　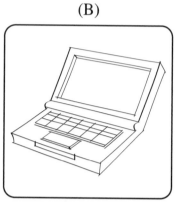　

For question number 1, please look at the three pictures. Question number 1, listen to the following message for Alan. What will Alan probably buy? Hi, Alan. It's Jane. I have to stay late at the office tonight to finish a report. Can you go buy some groceries we'll need for the weekend? Thanks so much. Bye.

翻譯

第一題，請看這三張圖。第一題，注意聆聽接下來給愛倫的留言。愛倫可能會買什麼？嗨，愛倫，我是珍。我要完成一份報告必須在辦公室待到很晚。你可以去買一些我們週末需要的雜貨嗎？謝謝你，再見。

解析

題目一開始就說明了這是一則留言。而留言通常是要告知某人某一件事、或是告知一個突發的狀況。了解題目是要問愛倫會買什麼東西之後，可以一邊聆聽接下來的留言內容，一邊掃視這三張圖。最後聽到 "groceries" 這個關鍵字，就知道珍是要請愛倫去買雜貨。

答案　　C

Question 2

(A)   (B)   (C)

For question number 2, please look at the three pictures. Question number 2, listen to the following announcement. Where will you probably hear it? Good day, ladies and gentlemen. We're having a special summer sale today. All summer dresses and T-shirts are half price now. Do not miss this good chance of getting some pretty clothes! Thank you for shopping with us today.

翻譯

第二題，請看這三張圖。第二題，注意聆聽接下來的廣播。你最有可能在哪裡聽到這則廣播？

早安，各位先生女士，我們今天正在舉行夏日特賣會。所有夏天的洋裝和 T 恤現在都是半價。請把握這個好機會，添購一些漂亮的衣服！謝謝你的蒞臨。

解析

題目一開始就說明了這是一則廣播。廣播有像是出現在各種場所的廣播，或各種情況、注意事項的廣播。題目一開始以 Where 開頭，所以我們可以知道這題要問的是地點。了解題目要問的問題後，聆聽接下來的廣播的同時，也要一邊掃視這三張圖片。廣播一開始就說：“We're having a special summer sale today.”，由此可判斷這是在商場裡的廣播，接著聽到 “summer dresses and T-shirts” 就可以知道這則廣播會在服飾店裡聽到。

答案　　B

Question 3

(A)　　　　　　(B)　　　　　　(C)

For question number 3, please look at the three pictures. Question number 3, listen to the following short talk. Which book did Donna Charles probably write?

Hello everyone. I'd like to introduce Donna Charles, the famous fiction writer. Her stories are enjoyed by children of all ages. When her books are published, they are immediately on the best-seller list.

翻 譯

第三題,請看這三張圖。第三題,注意聆聽接下來的簡短談話。哪一本書最有可能是唐娜‧查爾斯寫的?

大家好,我想向大家介紹一位有名的小說作家唐娜‧查爾斯。她寫的故事受到所有年齡層的孩童的喜愛。她的書一出版,就立即登上暢銷排行榜了。

解 析

題目一開始說明了這是一則簡短談話。這裡的簡短談話並不像第三部份簡短對話一樣,為兩人間一來一往的對答。這裡是敘述某事件,所以當聽到簡短談話時,最重要的就是要聽懂內容及掌握關鍵字。這一題若能掌握到 "writer"、"children" 及 "book" 就能了解這裡指的是童書,再來看看這三張圖,即能選出正確答案。

答 案　　A

Question 4

(A)   (B)   (C)

For question number 4, please look at the three pictures. Question number 4, David left a message for Judy. What will David do this evening?

Hi Judy. This is David. Sorry but I can't go to dinner with you this evening. I need to stay late at the library to finish a report for English class. Thanks, bye.

翻譯

第四題，請看這三張圖。第四題，大衛留了一則留言給茱蒂。大衛今天晚上會做什麼？
嗨，茱蒂。我是大衛。抱歉我今晚無法與你共進晚餐了。我要完成英文課的報告，所以需要在圖書館待到很晚。謝啦，再見。

解析

聽完題目問大衛最有可能做什麼後，就要注意聆聽大衛訴說自己的動向。首先要抓住關鍵字 "can't" 及後面的動作才知道大衛無法做什麼事。這裡大衛說自己無法與茱蒂共進晚餐，所以可以將選項 (A) 剔除。接著聽到他說 "stay late at the library"，掌握到 "library" 這個字就能選出選項 (C) 這個答案。

答案   C

Question 5

 (A)    (B)    (C)

For question number 5, please look at the three pictures. Question number 5, listen to the following short talk. What kind of job is Harry doing now? Harry has always been interested in fashion. He started designing clothes when he was in high school, and after studying fashion design at university, he became a successful fashion designer. His clothes are sold all over the world.

翻 譯

第五題，請看這三張圖。第五題，注意聆聽接下來的簡短談話。哈利現在的工作是什麼？

哈利一直都對時尚很有興趣。他在高中時就開始設計衣服，並且在大學讀了服裝設計之後，他成為一位成功的服裝設計師。他的衣服銷售到世界各地。

解 析

聽到題目以 "What kind of job" 問句開頭後，就知道接下來的談話內容是有關哈利工作的敘述。可以先留意一下圖片中人物的工作性質，再掌握住 "fashion"、"clothes" 及 "designer" 等關鍵字之後，即可選出選項 (B) 這個正確答案。

答 案   **B**

聽力測驗
實戰練習

準備好了嗎？接下來，12 個完全模擬全民
英檢聽力測驗的實戰練習單元，等著你來挑戰！

GEPT

Unit 1

本測驗分四個部份，全部都是單選題，共 30 題，作答時間約 20 分鐘。作答說明為中文，印在試題冊上並由音檔播出。

🎧 TRACK 05

第一部份：看圖辨義

共 5 題，每題請聽音檔播出題目和三個英語句子之後，選出與所看到的圖畫最相符的答案。每題只播出一遍。

A. Question 1

1. _____

B. Questions 2 and 3

San Min Elementary School

Student Information Form

Name: Bob Huang

Age: 10

Hobby: Movies, Music, Reading

2. _____

3. _____

C. Question 4

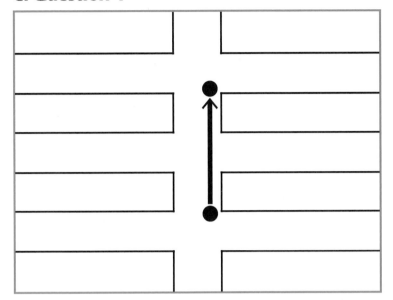

4. _____

D. Question 5

5. _____

第二部份：問答

共 10 題，每題請聽音檔播出的英語句子，再從試題冊上三個回答中，選出一個最適合的答案。每題只播出一遍。

_____ 6. (A) Thanks a lot.

(B) I am reading.

(C) Couldn't be better.

_____ 7. (A) I went to a movie last night.

(B) I play basketball and listen to music.

(C) Can you give me a few minutes?

_____ 8. (A) It's on my table.

(B) No, the river bank is ugly.

(C) I'm sorry. I don't know where it is.

_____ 9. (A) It's a long story.

(B) It's about time.

(C) About a week.

_____ 10. (A) Sure. This is my favorite.

(B) Of course. What is it?

(C) Yes, I think I have a fever.

_____ 11. (A) Tonight is a beautiful night.

(B) I like the tables very much.

(C) Well, how about tomorrow?

_____ 12. (A) Today is Sunday.

(B) I'll be glad to help.

(C) Sure, let's go see it.

_____ 13. (A) Sure, she will help.

(B) It's no big deal.

(C) No, I can't.

_____ 14. (A) All right. Just make sure it won't happen again.

(B) Sure. It is the best report that I have ever read.

(C) Thanks. I'll finish it on time.

_____ 15. (A) Sure, Mr. Smith.

(B) I'm sorry. I lost it.

(C) Nothing much.

TRACK 07

第三部份：簡短對話

共 10 題，每題請聽音檔播出一段對話和一個相關的問題後，再從試題冊上三個選項中，選出一個最適合的答案。每段對話和問題播出一遍。

_____ 16. (A) They work together and see each other every day.

(B) They don't know each other.

(C) They are friends, but they haven't seen each other a while ago.

_____ 17. (A) He plays instruments.

(B) He plays sports.

(C) He plays video games.

_____ 18. (A) A restroom.

(B) A block.

(C) A restaurant.

_____ 19. (A) He's talking to Jack.

(B) He's out for lunch.

(C) He's in a meeting.

_____ 20. (A) Wednesday at 2:00 p.m.

(B) Thursday at 1:00 p.m.

(C) Friday at 3:00 p.m.

_____ 21. (A) A party for her new apartment.

(B) A party for her birthday.

(C) A party for her new job.

_____ 22. (A) Buy some fruit.

   (B) Go to the train station.

   (C) Give Karen a call.

_____ 23. (A) He didn't know how to do it.

   (B) He was too tired to do it.

   (C) He forgot to hand it in.

_____ 24. (A) Tennis.

   (B) Baseball.

   (C) Basketball.

_____ 25. (A) Its service.

   (B) Its rooms.

   (C) Its food.

🎧 TRACK 08

第四部份：短文聽解

  共 5 題，每題有三個圖片選項。請聽音檔播出的題目，並選出一個最適合的圖片。每題播出一遍。

_____ 26.

(A)   (B)   (C)

_____ 30.

(A)   (B)   (C)

Unit 2

本測驗分四個部份，全部都是單選題，共 30 題，作答時間約 20 分鐘。作答說明為中文，印在試題冊上並由音檔播出。

🎧 TRACK 09

第一部份：看圖辨義

共 5 題，每題請聽音檔播出題目和三個英語句子之後，選出與所看到的圖畫最相符的答案。每題只播出一遍。

A. Question 1

1. _____

B. Questions 2 and 3

2. _____

3. _____

C. Question 4

4. _____

D. Question 5

5. _____

🎧 TRACK 10

第二部份：問答

共 10 題，每題請聽音檔播出的英語句子，再從試題冊上三個回答中，選出一個最適合的答案。每題只播出一遍。

_____ 6. (A) Wonderful.
(B) He is doing it now.
(C) I'm a student.

_____ 7. (A) English.
(B) Video games.
(C) French fries.

_____ 8. (A) No. The bank opens at 9:00 a.m.
(B) Sure. Walk straight and you'll see it on your right.
(C) It'll be the best way to get there.

_____ 9. (A) I have homework to do.
(B) I prefer this bag to that one.
(C) I walk home after school.

_____ 10. (A) It's none of your business.
(B) Your bicycle is wonderful.
(C) No problem.

_____ 11. (A) OK. I'll be there.
(B) No, tomorrow will be fine.
(C) Sure. What time?

_____ 12. (A) It was a good ride.
(B) That would be great!
(C) I think I'm right about it.

_____ 13. (A) Sure. Anytime.
(B) Sure. Here you go.
(C) Sure. Give me a call.

_____ 14. (A) Sure. Which book?

(B) Oh, I'm sorry.

(C) Yes, I have a voice mailbox.

_____ 15. (A) Fine, thank you, and you?

(B) No problem. Here you go.

(C) How's everything today?

第三部份：簡短對話

共 10 題，每題請聽音檔播出一段對話和一個相關的問題後，再從試題冊上三個選項中，選出一個最適合的答案。每段對話和問題播出一遍。

_____ 16. (A) Go to a hospital.

(B) Make a deal.

(C) Go to bed.

_____ 17. (A) Three.

(B) Four.

(C) Five.

_____ 18. (A) At a train station.

(B) In Taipei.

(C) At a bus stop.

_____ 19. (A) The woman.

(B) The woman's sister.

(C) The man.

_____ 20. (A) She has a fever.

(B) Her leg is broken.

(C) She has a pain in a tooth.

_____ 21. (A) They're going to finish a report together.

(B) They're going to have some desserts.

(C) They're going to a movie.

_____ 22. (A) She fixed the watch for the man.

(B) She lent her watch to the man.

(C) She bought a watch for the man.

_____ 23. (A) Schoolwork.

(B) Noise.

(C) Sports.

_____ 24. (A) Play football.

(B) Play video games.

(C) Watch a game.

_____ 25. (A) Its prices.

(B) Its food.

(C) Its service.

TRACK 12

第四部份：短文聽解

共 5 題，每題有三個圖片選項。請聽音檔播出的題目，並選出一個最適合的圖片。每題播出一遍。

_____ 26.

(A)    (B)    (C)

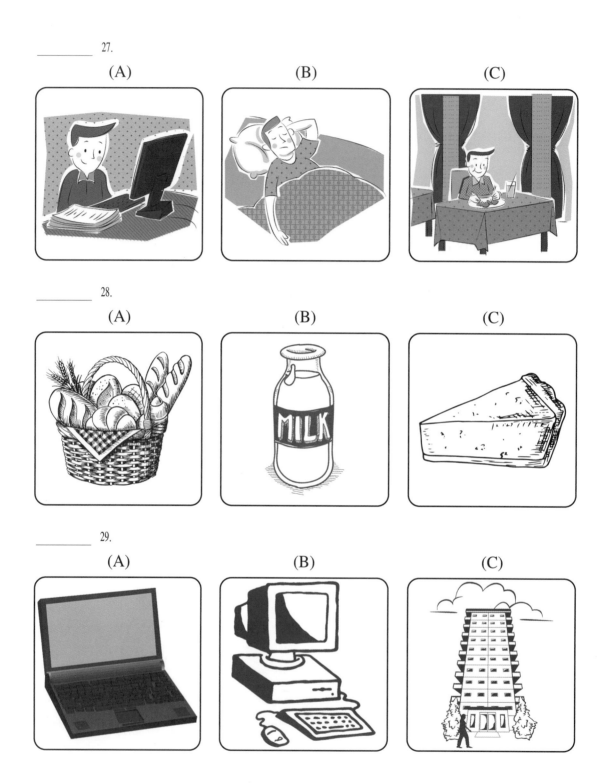

27.
(A)   (B)   (C)

28.
(A)   (B)   (C)

MILK

29.
(A)   (B)   (C)

_____ 30.

(A)

(B)

(C)

Unit 3

本測驗分四個部份，全部都是單選題，共 30 題，作答時間約 20 分鐘。作答說明為中文，印在試題冊上並由音檔播出。

🎧 TRACK 13

第一部份：看圖辨義

共 5 題，每題請聽音檔播出題目和三個英語句子之後，選出與所看到的圖畫最相符的答案。每題只播出一遍。

A. Question 1

1. _____

B. Questions 2 and 3

WARNING
Dangerous Animal

2. _____

3. _____

C. Question 4

4. _____

D. Question 5

5. _____

第二部份：問答

共 10 題，每題請聽音檔播出的英語句子，再從試題冊上三個回答中，選出一個最適合的答案。每題只播出一遍。

_____ 6. (A) It's 9:00 now.
(B) OK, I guess.
(C) It's going to rain.

_____ 7. (A) He is fine. Thanks.
(B) He is fixing my bike for me.
(C) He's a police officer.

_____ 8. (A) Yes. Thank you very much.
(B) The next bus stop is 500 meters away.
(C) Go straight. It's only two blocks down the road.

_____ 9. (A) Hold on. Let me get her for you.
(B) Sure. I'll call her back.
(C) Yes. Could you ask her to call Tom?

_____ 10. (A) Yes. Go ahead.
(B) Sure, no problem.
(C) No, thank you.

_____ 11. (A) I don't feel like cooking.
(B) I like cooking very much.
(C) It was really delicious.

_____ 12. (A) No, thank you.
(B) I'll call you later.
(C) You are welcome.

_____ 13. (A) Sounds great. I'll go, too.
(B) I'll be there for dinner.
(C) My pleasure.

14. (A) Fish is not my favorite food.

    (B) That's right. I like fishing very much.

    (C) Fishing is not crazy at all.

15. (A) I'm glad you asked.

    (B) Where is my answering machine?

    (C) Well, you'd better study harder.

第三部份：簡短對話

TRACK 15

共 10 題，每題請聽音檔播出一段對話和一個相關的問題後，再從試題冊上三個選項中，選出一個最適合的答案。每段對話和問題播出一遍。

16. (A) Think something in her mind.

    (B) Eat a slice of cake.

    (C) Lose some weight.

17. (A) Two.

    (B) Three.

    (C) Four.

18. (A) At the train station.

    (B) In the night market.

    (C) Near the hotel.

19. (A) The bedroom.

    (B) The living room.

    (C) The bathroom.

20. (A) For the next 10 minutes.

    (B) Around 5:00 p.m.

    (C) All day.

21. (A) She will attend another party.

    (B) She will have dinner with her mother.

    (C) She will be working late.

_____ 22. (A) The man took the woman home.

(B) They had dinner together.

(C) They went home by riding a bike.

_____ 23. (A) Drink.

(B) Service.

(C) Food.

_____ 24. (A) He knows the woman.

(B) He is unkind to others.

(C) He works with the man.

_____ 25. (A) They are not big enough.

(B) The shoes in a size 5 fit his feet.

(C) They don't suit him.

 TRACK 16

第四部份：短文聽解

　　共 5 題，每題有三個圖片選項。請聽音檔播出的題目，並選出一個最適合的圖片。每題播出一遍。

_____ 26.

(A)　　　　　　　　　　　(B)　　　　　　　　　　　(C)

_____ 27.

(A)   (B)   (C)

_____ 28.

(A)   (B)   (C)

_____ 29.

(A)   (B)   (C)

(A)

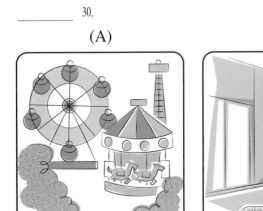

(B)

(C)

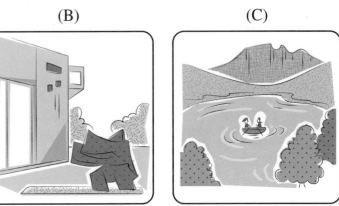

Unit 4

本測驗分四個部份，全部都是單選題，共 30 題，作答時間約 20 分鐘。作答說明為中文，印在試題冊上並由音檔播出。

🎧 TRACK 17

第一部份：看圖辨義

共 5 題，每題請聽音檔播出題目和三個英語句子之後，選出與所看到的圖畫最相符的答案。每題只播出一遍。

A. Question 1

1. _____

B. Question 2

2. _____

C. Questions 3 and 4

Time \ Doctor	Dr. Wall
3:00 p.m.	Lucy
4:00 p.m.	Ann
5:00 p.m.	Mark
6:00 p.m.	(Dinner)
7:00 p.m.	Jack

3. _____

4. _____

D. Question 5

5. _____

TRACK 18

第二部份：問答

　　共 10 題，每題請聽音檔播出的英語句子，再從試題冊上三個回答中，選出一個最適合的答案。每題只播出一遍。

_____ 6. (A) It's up to you.

　　　　　　(B) I'm up here.

　　　　　　(C) Nothing much.

_____ 7. (A) I am a taxi driver.

　　　　　　(B) I live in Taipei.

　　　　　　(C) You can't do that.

_____ 8. (A) Please have her call me back later.

　　　　　　(B) May I have your phone number?

　　　　　　(C) Hang on. I'll get her.

_____ 9. (A) Sure. What should I tell him?

　　　　　　(B) No, I will call him later.

　　　　　　(C) Good morning, Tom.

_____ 10. (A) Of course. I lost it.

　　　　　　(B) Yes, it's mine.

　　　　　　(C) Sure. Here you are.

_____ 11. (A) Great. I'll be there at 11.

　　　　　　(B) Yes, tomorrow night will be fine.

　　　　　　(C) No problem. What time?

_____ 12. (A) He is not coming.

　　　　　　(B) OK. They're really delicious.

　　　　　　(C) Why did you come?

_____ 13. (A) You are not welcome.

　　　　　　(B) That's nice of you to say so.

　　　　　　(C) No, that's mine.

_____ 14. (A) He is a great musician.

(B) What are you looking for?

(C) Gee, I'm really sorry.

_____ 15. (A) I'm fine, thank you.

(B) I think I did pretty well.

(C) I will do my best.

第三部份：簡短對話

共 10 題，每題請聽音檔播出一段對話和一個相關的問題後，再從試題冊上三個選項中，選出一個最適合的答案。每段對話和問題播出一遍。

_____ 16. (A) Last Friday.

(B) Last week.

(C) Last night.

_____ 17. (A) 79 years old.

(B) 80 years old.

(C) 81 years old.

_____ 18. (A) She wants to buy some food.

(B) She wants to find the train station.

(C) She wants to help the man.

_____ 19. (A) He wants to buy a book for the woman.

(B) He wants to borrow a book from the woman.

(C) He wants to lend the woman a book.

_____ 20. (A) 10:00 this morning.

(B) 10:30 this morning.

(C) 11:30 this morning.

_____ 21. (A) Eat some ice cream.

(B) Eat a piece of pie.

(C) Eat nothing.

_____ 22. (A) A hamburger only.

(B) A hamburger and fries.

(C) A hamburger, fries, and a Coke.

_____ 23. (A) Weather.

(B) Job.

(C) Traffic.

_____ 24. (A) A female singer.

(B) A male singer.

(C) A photo album.

_____ 25. (A) The color.

(B) The style.

(C) The price.

🎧 TRACK 20

第四部份：短文聽解

共 5 題，每題有三個圖片選項。請聽音檔播出的題目，並選出一個最適合的圖片。每題播出一遍。

_____ 26.

(A)   (B)   (C)

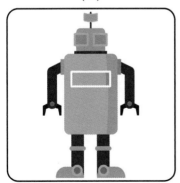  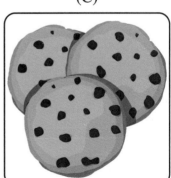

27.

(A)   (B)    (C)

lost-and-found

emergency exit

INFORMATION

28.

(A)   (B)    (C)

$

29.

(A)   (B)    (C)

_____ 30.

(A)

(B)

(C)

Unit 5

本測驗分四個部份，全部都是單選題，共 30 題，作答時間約 20 分鐘。作答說明為中文，印在試題冊上並由音檔播出。

TRACK 21

共 5 題，每題請聽音檔播出題目和三個英語句子之後，選出與所看到的圖畫最相符的答案。每題只播出一遍。

A. Question 1

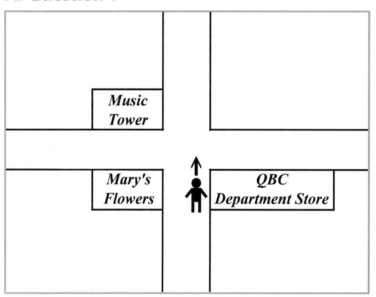

1. _____

B. Questions 2 and 3

Trains from Taipei

To Taichung ················8:20

To Tainan ················9:45

To Kaohsiung ·········10:00

To Hualien ···············11:10

2. _____

3. _____

C. Questions 4 and 5

4. _____

5. _____

第二部份：問答　　　　　　　　　　　🎧 TRACK 22

　　共 10 題，每題請聽音檔播出的英語句子，再從試題冊上三個回答中，選出一個最適合的答案。每題只播出一遍。

_____ 6. (A) I have been to Tainan.

(B) Nice to meet you.

(C) Not bad at all. And you?

_____ 7. (A) The sooner the better.

(B) I'm sorry to hear that.

(C) You should do your homework after school.

_____ 8. (A) I've never heard of that place.

(B) That's OK. I'll ask someone else.

(C) Sure. You won't miss it.

_____ 9. (A) Sure. You can eat what you want.

(B) Well, but I'm on a diet.

(C) Can I have a bite of your cake?

_____ 10. (A) Yes, I wanted the radio.

(B) Sure, no problem.

(C) No, thanks.

_____ 11. (A) Why not?

(B) Riding a motorcycle is fun.

(C) Me, too.

_____ 12. (A) I'm glad you are.

(B) Do you really like it?

(C) Oh, thank you so much.

_____ 13. (A) It was nothing.

(B) Thank you very much.

(C) You can say that again!

_____ 14. (A) I prefer watching TV to reading a book.

(B) I was sick yesterday.

(C) I like it very much.

_____ 15. (A) I'd like to, but I have football practice today.

(B) It was a good movie.

(C) Sure. Go straight and turn right, and you'll see it.

TRACK 23

第三部份：簡短對話

共 10 題，每題請聽音檔播出一段對話和一個相關的問題後，再從試題冊上三個選項中，選出一個最適合的答案。每段對話和問題播出一遍。

_____ 16. (A) Vendors on West Street.

(B) Where they live.

(C) When they first met.

_____ 17. (A) Taking a bus is more convenient.

(B) The man doesn't like to walk.

(C) The man doesn't have much time.

18. (A) 784-7586.

(B) 784-7568.

(C) 786-7586.

19. (A) In a hotel.

(B) In a department store.

(C) In a coffee shop.

20. (A) Tomorrow.

(B) Later this month.

(C) Next month.

21. (A) She'd like to have sugar and cream in it.

(B) She didn't want sugar or cream in it.

(C) She'd like to have black tea.

22. (A) He wants to work there.

(B) He will get there at 10.

(C) He wants to book a table.

23. (A) Traffic.

(B) Education.

(C) Environment.

24. (A) Too big.

(B) Too small.

(C) Too expensive.

25. (A) Love stories.

(B) Ghost stories.

(C) History stories.

第四部份：短文聽解

共 5 題，每題有三個圖片選項。請聽音檔播出的題目，並選出一個最適合的圖片。每題播出一遍。

_____ 26.

(A)   (B)   (C)

_____ 27.

(A)   (B)   (C)

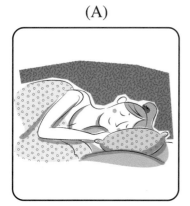

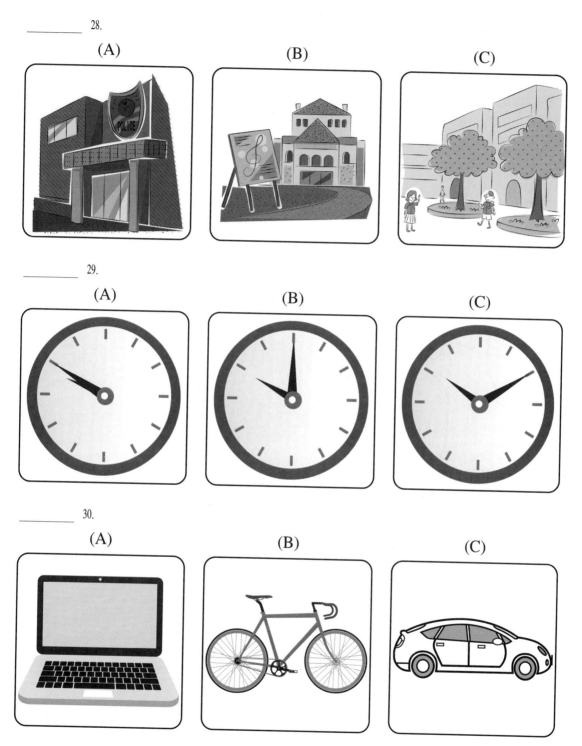

28.　(A)　(B)　(C)

29.　(A)　(B)　(C)

30.　(A)　(B)　(C)

Unit 6

本測驗分四個部份，全部都是單選題，共 30 題，作答時間約 20 分鐘。作答說明為中文，印在試題冊上並由音檔播出。

🎧 TRACK 25

第一部份：看圖辨義

共 5 題，每題請聽音檔播出題目和三個英語句子之後，選出與所看到的圖畫最相符的答案。每題只播出一遍。

A. Question 1

1. _____

B. Questions 2 and 3

Basketball Game

Taipei Bears vs. Shanghai Tigers

| 106 | 89 |

2. _____

3. _____

C. Question 4

4. _____

D. Question 5

5. _____

第二部份：問答

　　共 10 題，每題請聽音檔播出的英語句子，再從試題冊上三個回答中，選出一個最適合的答案。每題只播出一遍。

_____ 6. (A) Fine, thanks. How about you?
　　　　　　(B) The weather is beautiful.
　　　　　　(C) You are welcome.

_____ 7. (A) I enjoy my work very much.
　　　　　　(B) I work in a bookstore.
　　　　　　(C) I work five days a week.

_____ 8. (A) The next movie will begin at 2:30.
　　　　　　(B) It's NT$250 for one person.
　　　　　　(C) Go down the stairs to B1.

_____ 9. (A) She's not in now.
　　　　　　(B) Speaking.
　　　　　　(C) No, thanks.

_____ 10. (A) No, not at all.
　　　　　　(B) Yes, please.
　　　　　　(C) No, it was yesterday afternoon.

_____ 11. (A) Sounds great.
　　　　　　(B) Dinner was good.
　　　　　　(C) He will come over tomorrow.

_____ 12. (A) Yes, I want orange juice.
　　　　　　(B) No, I'd like it black.
　　　　　　(C) That'd be nice. Thank you.

_____ 13. (A) Yes, I do. Chocolate is my favorite.
　　　　　　(B) The cake is too sweet.
　　　　　　(C) Pass the sugar, please.

_____ 14. (A) Never mind.

(B) Be my guest.

(C) It's hard to say.

_____ 15. (A) Sure, Ms. Lin.

(B) No, never mind.

(C) Yes, you're right.

🎧 TRACK 27

第三部份：簡短對話

共 10 題，每題請聽音檔播出一段對話和一個相關的問題後，再從試題冊上三個選項中，選出一個最適合的答案。每段對話和問題播出一遍。

_____ 16. (A) Cakes.

(B) Ice cream.

(C) Nothing.

_____ 17. (A) To buy him a drink.

(B) To send a mail for him.

(C) To get some food for him.

_____ 18. (A) The woman will tell the man where Louis is.

(B) The woman will call Louis right away.

(C) The woman will take a message for Louis.

_____ 19. (A) Drive the woman to the airport.

(B) Take the woman out for a ride.

(C) Pick up the woman at the airport.

_____ 20. (A) A match.

(B) A speech.

(C) A test.

_____ 21. (A) He slept late.

(B) He was caught in heavy traffic.

(C) He forgot to set the alarm.

_____ 22. (A) In a bakery.

(B) In a furniture store.

(C) In a stationery store.

_____ 23. (A) Work.

(B) Health.

(C) Hospital.

_____ 24. (A) Wrong color.

(B) Wrong style.

(C) Wrong size.

_____ 25. (A) He thinks the dress doesn't match the woman's shoes.

(B) He thinks the color of the dress isn't right for the woman.

(C) He thinks the dress is too expensive.

第四部份：短文聽解

🎧 TRACK 28

共 5 題，每題有三個圖片選項。請聽音檔播出的題目，並選出一個最適合的圖片。每題播出一遍。

_____ 26.

(A)

(B)

(C)

_____ 27.

(A)

(B)

(C)

_____ 28.

(A)

(B)

(C)

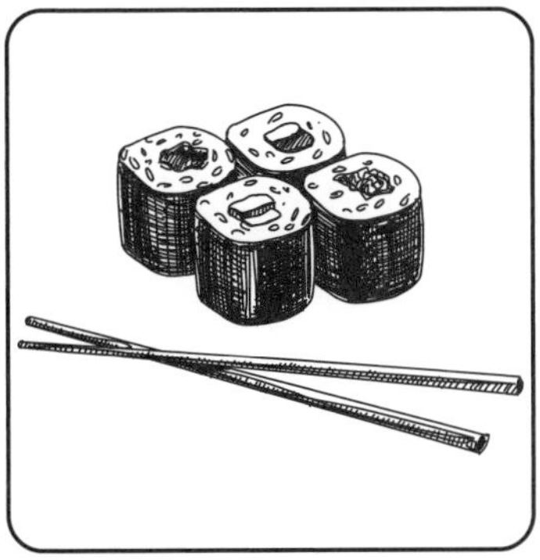

_____ 29.

(A)

(B)

(C)

30.

(A)

(B)

(C)

本測驗分四個部份，全部都是單選題，共 30 題，作答時間約 20 分鐘。作答說明為中文，印在試題冊上並由音檔播出。

🎧 TRACK 29

第一部份：看圖辨義

　　共 5 題，每題請聽音檔播出題目和三個英語句子之後，選出與所看到的圖畫最相符的答案。每題只播出一遍。

A. Question 1

1. _____

B. Questions 2 and 3

2. _____

3. _____

C. Question 4

4. _____

D. Question 5

5. _____

🎧 TRACK 30

共 10 題，每題請聽音檔播出的英語句子，再從試題冊上三個回答中，選出一個最適合的答案。每題只播出一遍。

6. (A) Nothing special.
   (B) What day is today?
   (C) I am studying.

7. (A) Eighteen.
   (B) August.
   (C) 1988.

8. (A) Sure. They're on the third floor.
   (B) The gift shop is next to the coffee shop.
   (C) I'm sorry. I didn't see any children here.

9. (A) I need some sleep now.
   (B) No wonder you look so tired.
   (C) Thank you for buying me a cup of coffee.

10. (A) Yes. Can I see Mr. Lin today?
    (B) Yes. He is right there.
    (C) No, would you like to leave a message?

11. (A) You are welcome.
    (B) Sure. It sounds like fun.
    (C) Don't mention it.

12. (A) Nice to meet you.
    (B) No, they're very happy.
    (C) Sure. Why not?

13. (A) Thank you so much.
    (B) That's OK.
    (C) It's not my fault.

_____ 14. (A) Are you ready to order?

(B) Oh, I'm sorry. I got it wrong.

(C) There is no ice.

_____ 15. (A) There will be no one there.

(B) On May 15.

(C) In the Lowe Theater.

第三部份：簡短對話

共 10 題，每題請聽音檔播出一段對話和一個相關的問題後，再從試題冊上三個選項中，選出一個最適合的答案。每段對話和問題播出一遍。

_____ 16. (A) Her little brother.

(B) Her little sister.

(C) Her little daughter.

_____ 17. (A) Where to take the bus.

(B) What bus stops at the National Theater.

(C) How long the bus takes to the National Theater.

_____ 18. (A) He is in the hospital.

(B) He is making a phone call.

(C) He is at home.

_____ 19. (A) One.

(B) Two.

(C) Three.

_____ 20. (A) She doesn't like coffee.

(B) She has to see her dentist.

(C) She is afraid of the man.

_____ 21. (A) Orange juice.

(B) Cold beer.

(C) Water.

22. (A) She lost Ted's umbrella.

    (B) She forgot to bring Ted's umbrella.

    (C) She didn't buy Ted a new umbrella.

23. (A) The smell of burnt food.

    (B) The smoke from a factory.

    (C) The smoke in a non-smoking place.

24. (A) A department store.

    (B) A restaurant.

    (C) A bookstore.

25. (A) She has small eyes.

    (B) She wears red clothes.

    (C) Her hair color is light brown.

🎧 TRACK 32

第四部份：短文聽解

　　共 5 題，每題有三個圖片選項。請聽音檔播出的題目，並選出一個最適合的圖片。每題播出一遍。

26.

(A)　　　　　　　　(B)　　　　　　　　(C)

_____ 27.

(A)   (B)   (C)

_____ 28.

(A)   (B)   (C)

_____ 29.

(A)   (B)   (C)

_____ 30.

(A)　　　　　　　　　(B)　　　　　　　　　(C)

 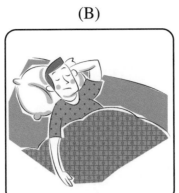 

Unit 8

本測驗分四個部份，全部都是單選題，共 30 題，作答時間約 20 分鐘。作答說明為中文，印在試題冊上並由音檔播出。

🎧 TRACK 33

第一部份：看圖辨義

共 5 題，每題請聽音檔播出題目和三個英語句子之後，選出與所看到的圖畫最相符的答案。每題只播出一遍。

A. Question 1

1. _____

B. Question 2

2. _____

C. Questions 3 and 4

BEST PRICE!

Buy One And

Get One FREE

3. _____

4. _____

D. Question 5

5. _____

第二部份：問答

　　共 10 題，每題請聽音檔播出的英語句子，再從試題冊上三個回答中，選出一個最適合的答案。每題只播出一遍。

_____ 6. (A) Don't mention it.
　　　　　　　(B) I must apologize.
　　　　　　　(C) I wish I could.

_____ 7. (A) 2005.
　　　　　　　(B) Summer.
　　　　　　　(C) July 4th.

_____ 8. (A) Yes. What would you like to order?
　　　　　　　(B) No, it's quite close.
　　　　　　　(C) Sure. Where do you want to go?

_____ 9. (A) No, not at all.
　　　　　　　(B) I may not go.
　　　　　　　(C) Don't do that.

_____ 10. (A) Yes, I'm a teacher.
　　　　　　　(B) I don't like him.
　　　　　　　(C) I'll give you a hand.

_____ 11. (A) I'd like some tea, please.
　　　　　　　(B) Sure. When will it be?
　　　　　　　(C) How did you get the concert tickets?

_____ 12. (A) Sure. Here you are.
　　　　　　　(B) You're welcome.
　　　　　　　(C) No, thank you. I'm really full.

_____ 13. (A) All right, I'll go with you.
　　　　　　　(B) I missed the train.
　　　　　　　(C) You can save a lot of time.

_____ 14. (A) Sure, I'll be right back.

(B) Hot water will be fine.

(C) Coffee, please.

_____ 15. (A) I usually walk to school.

(B) Me, too. Why don't we take a taxi?

(C) Yes, it's quite crowded on the bus.

🎧 TRACK 35

第三部份：簡短對話

　　共 10 題，每題請聽音檔播出一段對話和一個相關的問題後，再從試題冊上三個選項中，選出一個最適合的答案。每段對話和問題播出一遍。

_____ 16. (A) Cross over the road.

(B) Take this bus.

(C) Ask another person.

_____ 17. (A) Ask Fred to come to the phone.

(B) Have Helen call Fred.

(C) Leave a message for Fred.

_____ 18. (A) A new car.

(B) A new computer.

(C) A new game.

_____ 19. (A) This morning.

(B) This afternoon.

(C) Tomorrow afternoon.

_____ 20. (A) Go shopping.

(B) Go to a party.

(C) Go to a movie.

_____ 21. (A) A piece of strawberry cake.

(B) A piece of cheesecake.

(C) Nothing.

_____ 22. (A) Games.

(B) Pets.

(C) Books.

_____ 23. (A) The man should stop complaining.

(B) The man should quit his job.

(C) The man should do some exercise.

_____ 24. (A) Move to a new apartment.

(B) Do a favor for the woman.

(C) Stay at home.

_____ 25. (A) A white dress.

(B) The man's wife.

(C) The woman's looks.

🎧 TRACK 36

第四部份：短文聽解

共 5 題，每題有三個圖片選項。請聽音檔播出的題目，並選出一個最適合的圖片。每題播出一遍。

_____ 26.

(A) (B) (C)

_____ 27.

(A)   (B)   (C)

_____ 28.

(A)   (B)   (C)

_____ 29.

(A)   (B)   (C)

_____ 30.

(A)

(B)

(C)

Unit 9

本測驗分四個部份，全部都是單選題，共 30 題，作答時間約 20 分鐘。作答說明為中文，印在試題冊上並由音檔播出。

🎧 TRACK 37

第一部份：看圖辨義

共 5 題，每題請聽音檔播出題目和三個英語句子之後，選出與所看到的圖畫最相符的答案。每題只播出一遍。

A. Question 1

1. _____

B. Question 2

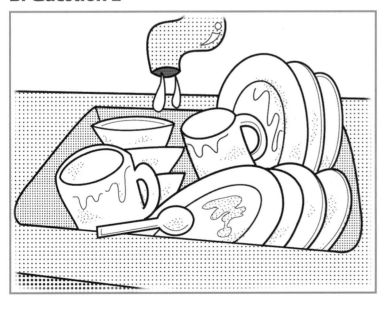

2. _____

C. Question 3

3. _____

D. Question 4

4. _____

E. Question 5

US POSTAGE

PAID

NO STAMP REQUIRED

5. _____

🎧 TRACK 38

第二部份：問答

共 10 題，每題請聽音檔播出的英語句子，再從試題冊上三個回答中，選出一個最適合的答案。每題只播出一遍。

_____ 6. (A) Really? I thought Taiwan is a small island.

(B) I've never been abroad.

(C) I don't like Taiwanese food.

_____ 7. (A) It is around the corner.

(B) It is going to be on time.

(C) The station closes at 11 p.m.

_____ 8. (A) No, thanks.

(B) No, I don't.

(C) Sorry. He is not in.

_____ 9. (A) I wonder how.

(B) It is useful.

(C) Of course.

10. (A) Much better.

(B) No, it won't help.

(C) I can tell you why.

11. (A) Thanks for your help.

(B) I was tired last Sunday.

(C) Yes. What time?

12. (A) Thanks a million.

(B) It's my pleasure.

(C) How kind of you.

13. (A) Sorry. I'll turn it down right away.

(B) He is not a musician.

(C) Yes. You are welcome.

14. (A) The work is wonderful.

(B) Thanks a lot.

(C) OK. I'll do that.

15. (A) I think they look great.

(B) They are size 12.

(C) I bought them for my mother.

TRACK 39

第三部份：簡短對話

　　共 10 題，每題請聽音檔播出一段對話和一個相關的問題後，再從試題冊上三個選項中，選出一個最適合的答案。每段對話和問題播出一遍。

16. (A) Twelve.

(B) Ten.

(C) Eight.

17. (A) Check the flight schedule for her.

(B) Fly to Tokyo on October 6th.

(C) Book two bus tickets to Taipei.

_____ 18. (A) Tonight.

      (B) 8 o'clock.

      (C) Next month.

_____ 19. (A) Her nose is running.

      (B) She has a fever.

      (C) She wants to drive.

_____ 20. (A) He's going to solve a problem.

      (B) He and Chuck are going to a movie.

      (C) He is going to a party.

_____ 21. (A) Chinese food.

      (B) Japanese food.

      (C) Korean food.

_____ 22. (A) Where to buy a new book.

      (B) How to make it up to the man.

      (C) When to apologize for the mistake.

_____ 23. (A) It was lost on the bus.

      (B) It was left at home.

      (C) It was on the teacher's desk.

_____ 24. (A) Clothes.

      (B) Exercise.

      (C) Food.

_____ 25. (A) The coat is too expensive.

      (B) The size is not right.

      (C) The color is wrong.

第四部份：短文聽解

　　共 5 題，每題有三個圖片選項。請聽音檔播出的題目，並選出一個最適合的圖片。每題播出一遍。

_____ 26.

(A)    (B)    (C)

_____ 27.

(A)    (B)    (C)

_____ 28.

(A)

(B)

(C)

_____ 29.

(A)

(B)

SanMin Cinema

(C)

2nd STREET

_____ 30.

(A)

(B)

(C)

Unit 10

本測驗分四個部份，全部都是單選題，共 30 題，作答時間約 20 分鐘。作答說明為中文，印在試題冊上並由音檔播出。

TRACK 41

第一部份：看圖辨義

共 5 題，每題請聽音檔播出題目和三個英語句子之後，選出與所看到的圖畫最相符的答案。每題只播出一遍。

A. Questions 1 and 2

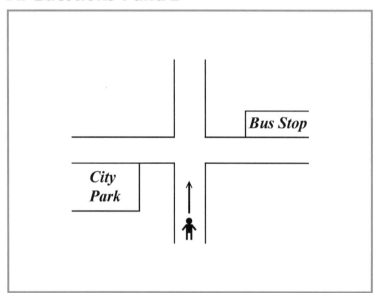

1. _____

2. _____

B. Questions 3 and 4

SAVE UP TO **40%**

ON SELECT CAMERAS

EVERY WEEK

3. _____

4. _____

C. Question 5

5. _____

 TRACK 42

第二部份：問答

　　共 10 題，每題請聽音檔播出的英語句子，再從試題冊上三個回答中，選出一個最適合的答案。每題只播出一遍。

_____ 6. (A) Yes. My father is a doctor.

(B) No. I am an only child.

(C) Yes. My brother and sister are students, too.

_____ 7. (A) My father will.

(B) It's 2:30 p.m.

(C) I'm going to Japan.

_____ 8. (A) I'm not leaving.

(B) Yes. Please tell her Mary called.

(C) Thanks for calling.

_____ 9. (A) You're welcome.

(B) Sure. Here you are.

(C) I'd love to.

_____ 10. (A) I had a great time last night.

(B) How about tomorrow morning around 10?

(C) I'm sorry. He is my father.

_____ 11. (A) No, thanks. I have work to do.

(B) I'm sorry. I'm new in town.

(C) Yes, this is my shop.

_____ 12. (A) Park Theater.

(B) In 15 minutes.

(C) I like it.

_____ 13. (A) How much is it?

(B) Where is my coke?

(C) For here or to go?

_____ 14. (A) Sorry, I'll change it for you.

(B) Sorry, it is out of order.

(C) Sorry, the place is closed.

_____ 15. (A) All right, I'll do that.

(B) You did a great job. Keep going.

(C) Thanks. I'm so happy to hear that.

第三部份：簡短對話　　　　　　　　　　　🎧 TRACK 43

　　共 10 題，每題請聽音檔播出一段對話和一個相關的問題後，再從試題冊上三個選項中，選出一個最適合的答案。每段對話和問題播出一遍。

_____ 16. (A) A crime.

(B) A book.

(C) A drama.

_____ 17. (A) Take the woman to the movie theater.

(B) Ask somebody else.

(C) Show the woman his movie ticket.

_____ 18. (A) 12 o'clock.

(B) 2 o'clock.

(C) 3 o'clock.

_____ 19. (A) She didn't like the size.

(B) She didn't like the color.

(C) She didn't like the style.

_____ 20. (A) She doesn't like the movie.

(B) She is a Japanese.

(C) She will be in class.

_____ 21. (A) They are friends.

(B) Shrimps are good.

(C) In a restaurant.

_____ 22. (A) He went out with Lucy.

(B) He went to the KTV.

(C) He went to a birthday party.

_____ 23. (A) A teacher and a student.

(B) A boss and a worker.

(C) A customer and a waitress.

_____ 24. (A) 50 dollars.

(B) 610 dollars.

(C) 560 dollars.

_____ 25. (A) In a classroom.

(B) In a store.

(C) At home.

第四部份：短文聽解

共 5 題，每題有三個圖片選項。請聽音檔播出的題目，並選出一個最適合的圖片。每題播出一遍。

_____ 26.

(A)    (B)    (C)

_____ 27.

(A)    (B) 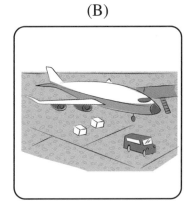   (C)

28.

(A)   (B)   (C)

29.

(A)   (B)   (C)

30.

(A)   (B)   (C)

Unit 11

本測驗分四個部份，全部都是單選題，共 30 題，作答時間約 20 分鐘。作答說明為中文，印在試題冊上並由音檔播出。

🎧 TRACK 45

第一部份：看圖辨義

共 5 題，每題請聽音檔播出題目和三個英語句子之後，選出與所看到的圖畫最相符的答案。每題只播出一遍。

A. Question 1

1. ＿＿＿＿＿＿＿＿

B. Questions 2 and 3

2. ＿＿＿＿＿＿＿＿

3. ＿＿＿＿＿＿＿＿

C. Question 4

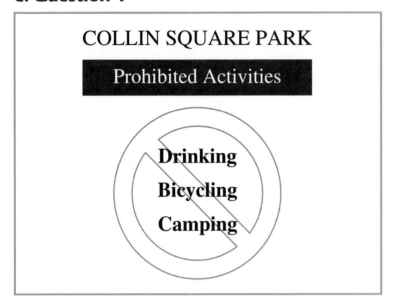

COLLIN SQUARE PARK

Prohibited Activities

Drinking

Bicycling

Camping

4. _____

D. Question 5

5. _____

第二部份：問答

共 10 題，每題請聽音檔播出的英語句子，再從試題冊上三個回答中，選出一個最適合的答案。每題只播出一遍。

_____ 6. (A) Sorry, I didn't mean it.

(B) What's up?

(C) OK. Thanks!

_____ 7. (A) OK, I'm leaving now.

(B) Yes, orange juice will be fine.

(C) That'd be great. Thanks.

_____ 8. (A) How's everything?

(B) I'm glad to see you again.

(C) Oh, you shouldn't have.

_____ 9. (A) Yes, I left home 8 years ago.

(B) Oh, I got some work to do.

(C) I was wearing a T-shirt.

_____ 10. (A) Thank you very much.

(B) I'm sorry. I'll change that for you.

(C) Well, I'll cook later.

_____ 11. (A) I'm sorry. I won't do it again.

(B) Yes. He has a cold.

(C) Sure. See you tomorrow.

_____ 12. (A) Yes, I'm lost.

(B) No, I will buy 20 pounds.

(C) Yes. Isn't it wonderful?

_____ 13. (A) I have a date later. How about tomorrow?

(B) Don't be silly. Who told you that?

(C) That's right. I'm going to move tomorrow.

_____ 14. (A) I've known her since we were kids.

(B) She is in my class.

(C) She's the one in the white dress.

_____ 15. (A) Tomorrow night will be fine.

(B) I stayed at home.

(C) That was the last time I saw her.

第三部份：簡短對話　　　　　　　　　　🎧 TRACK 47

　　共 10 題，每題請聽音檔播出一段對話和一個相關的問題後，再從試題冊上三個選項中，選出一個最適合的答案。每段對話和問題播出一遍。

_____ 16. (A) Her aunt is coming.

(B) She'll practice basketball.

(C) She doesn't like the man.

_____ 17. (A) Pizza.

(B) Salad.

(C) Nothing.

_____ 18. (A) She made fun of him.

(B) She lent him the motorcycle.

(C) She took him to the beach.

_____ 19. (A) He lost the book.

(B) He bought another book.

(C) He forgot to bring the book.

_____ 20. (A) A policeman and a driver.

(B) A waiter and a customer.

(C) A teacher and a student.

_____ 21. (A) They are lining up.

(B) They are going home.

(C) They are waiting for a star.

_____ 22. (A) A student.

　　　　　　(B) A teacher.

　　　　　　(C) A dentist.

_____ 23. (A) It is small.

　　　　　　(B) The rent is cheap.

　　　　　　(C) It is near the bus stop.

_____ 24. (A) In a train station.

　　　　　　(B) In a bookstore.

　　　　　　(C) In a watch shop.

_____ 25. (A) He forgot to do his homework.

　　　　　　(B) He didn't study for the exam.

　　　　　　(C) He wasn't able to answer the question.

第四部份：短文聽解

　　共 5 題，每題有三個圖片選項。請聽音檔播出的題目，並選出一個最適合的圖片。每題播出一遍。

_____ 26.

(A) (B) (C)

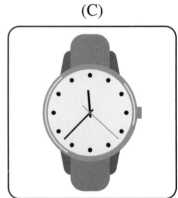

27.

(A)

(B)

(C)

28.

(A)

(B)

(C)

29.

(A)

(B)

(C)

30.

(A)

(B)

(C)

Unit 12

本測驗分四個部份，全部都是單選題，共 30 題，作答時間約 20 分鐘。作答說明為中文，印在試題冊上並由音檔播出。

🎧 TRACK 49

第一部份：看圖辨義

　　共 5 題，每題請聽音檔播出題目和三個英語句子之後，選出與所看到的圖畫最相符的答案。每題只播出一遍。

A. Questions 1 and 2

> **You are invited to celebrate the wedding of Mary Fox & John Wolf**
> on Saturday afternoon
> June the 15th
> at 5 o'clock

1. ＿＿＿＿＿＿＿

2. ＿＿＿＿＿＿＿

B. Question 3

Mary,

Meet you in the theater at 7 p.m.

John

3. ＿＿＿＿＿＿＿

C. Question 4

4. _____

D. Question 5

5. _____

第二部份：問答

　共 10 題，每題請聽音檔播出的英語句子，再從試題冊上三個回答中，選出一個最適合的答案。每題只播出一遍。

_____ 6. (A) The game is over.

(B) Sure. That would be fun.

(C) Yes, enjoy your food.

_____ 7. (A) Yes, I don't.

(B) No, I'd like more.

(C) No, thanks. I'm full.

_____ 8. (A) I'm sorry.

(B) It was nothing.

(C) We're late.

_____ 9. (A) You are welcome.

(B) Thank you.

(C) That's OK.

_____ 10. (A) Really? I hate music.

(B) How do you like the food?

(C) I'm really sorry about that.

_____ 11. (A) I'm not free tonight.

(B) I'm going home now.

(C) I like to exercise.

_____ 12. (A) I don't know you, either.

(B) Oh, thank you!

(C) Let me show you how to write.

_____ 13. (A) I don't like Chinese food.

(B) I really had a great time.

(C) Japan is close to Taiwan.

14. (A) Yes. It is my dog.

    (B) He is my brother.

    (C) They are my classmates.

15. (A) Coffee, please.

    (B) Medium, please.

    (C) Yes, please.

第三部份：簡短對話

　　共 10 題，每題請聽音檔播出一段對話和一個相關的問題後，再從試題冊上三個選項中，選出一個最適合的答案。每段對話和問題播出一遍。

16. (A) They will go fishing.

    (B) They will go to a movie.

    (C) They will go shopping.

17. (A) A hamburger and a coke.

    (B) French fries and a coke.

    (C) A hamburger and French fries.

18. (A) She took him to dinner.

    (B) She helped him with his paper.

    (C) She gave him a high score.

19. (A) Talk on the phone.

    (B) Turn down the volume.

    (C) Turn on the TV.

20. (A) At the airport.

    (B) At the train station.

    (C) At the bus station.

21. (A) Barbara's brother.

    (B) Barbara's boyfriend.

    (C) Barbara's teacher.

_____ 22. (A) Weather.
　　　　(B) Clothes.
　　　　(C) Umbrella.

_____ 23. (A) Eggs.
　　　　(B) Apples.
　　　　(C) Carrots.

_____ 24. (A) Cook French food for the woman.
　　　　(B) Buy the woman dinner.
　　　　(C) Lend the woman some money.

_____ 25. (A) A driver.
　　　　(B) A writer.
　　　　(C) A waiter.

🎧 TRACK 52

第四部份：短文聽解

　　共 5 題，每題有三個圖片選項。請聽音檔播出的題目，並選出一個最適合的圖片。每題播出一遍。

_____ 26.
(A)　　　　　　　　(B)　　　　　　　　(C)

_____ 27.

(A)   (B)   (C)

_____ 28.

(A)   (B)   (C)

_____ 29.

(A)   (B)   (C)

_____ 30.

(A)    (B)    (C)

Answer Key

Unit 1

1. B	2. B	3. A	4. C	5. B	6. C	7. B	8. C	9. C	10. B
11. C	12. C	13. B	14. A	15. A	16. C	17. B	18. C	19. C	20. C
21. B	22. B	23. B	24. B	25. A	26. A	27. B	28. B	29. C	30. B

Unit 2

1. C	2. A	3. B	4. A	5. C	6. A	7. A	8. B	9. A	10. C
11. A	12. B	13. A	14. B	15. B	16. C	17. C	18. A	19. C	20. C
21. B	22. C	23. B	24. C	25. B	26. B	27. A	28. B	29. A	30. B

Unit 3

1. B	2. C	3. B	4. A	5. B	6. B	7. C	8. C	9. C	10. B
11. C	12. A	13. C	14. B	15. C	16. C	17. B	18. C	19. C	20. C
21. B	22. B	23. C	24. C	25. A	26. C	27. C	28. B	29. C	30. C

Unit 4

1. C	2. B	3. B	4. B	5. C	6. C	7. A	8. C	9. A	10. C
11. A	12. B	13. B	14. C	15. B	16. C	17. A	18. C	19. B	20. A
21. A	22. B	23. A	24. A	25. C	26. B	27. A	28. B	29. C	30. C

Unit 5

1. C	2. A	3. C	4. A	5. C	6. C	7. A	8. B	9. B	10. B
11. A	12. C	13. A	14. C	15. A	16. B	17. C	18. B	19. B	20. B
21. B	22. C	23. A	24. C	25. A	26. A	27. A	28. A	29. B	30. C

Unit 6

1. C	2. A	3. A	4. C	5. A	6. A	7. B	8. C	9. B	10. A
11. A	12. C	13. A	14. A	15. A	16. C	17. B	18. C	19. A	20. C
21. B	22. B	23. B	24. C	25. B	26. C	27. A	28. B	29. A	30. B

Unit 7

1. B	2. A	3. A	4. A	5. C	6. A	7. A	8. A	9. B	10. A
11. B	12. C	13. B	14. B	15. B	16. B	17. B	18. A	19. A	20. B
21. C	22. A	23. C	24. B	25. B	26. B	27. A	28. C	29. C	30. B

Unit 8

1. B	2. C	3. B	4. C	5. A	6. A	7. C	8. C	9. A	10. B
11. B	12. C	13. B	14. A	15. B	16. A	17. B	18. B	19. C	20. C
21. A	22. B	23. B	24. B	25. B	26. A	27. C	28. A	29. A	30. C

Unit 9

1. C	2. A	3. C	4. C	5. B	6. B	7. A	8. C	9. C	10. A
11. C	12. B	13. A	14. C	15. A	16. B	17. A	18. A	19. B	20. B
21. A	22. B	23. B	24. A	25. B	26. C	27. A	28. B	29. B	30. A

Unit 10

1. C	2. C	3. A	4. B	5. B	6. B	7. A	8. B	9. C	10. B
11. A	12. B	13. C	14. A	15. C	16. B	17. B	18. A	19. B	20. C
21. C	22. A	23. A	24. C	25. B	26. B	27. A	28. C	29. C	30. C

Unit 11

1. B	2. B	3. B	4. A	5. A	6. C	7. C	8. C	9. B	10. B
11. B	12. C	13. A	14. C	15. B	16. A	17. B	18. B	19. C	20. B
21. C	22. C	23. C	24. C	25. C	26. A	27. C	28. C	29. C	30. C

Unit 12

1. C	2. A	3. C	4. B	5. B	6. B	7. C	8. B	9. C	10. C
11. C	12. B	13. B	14. B	15. B	16. B	17. A	18. B	19. B	20. B
21. C	22. A	23. B	24. B	25. C	26. B	27. B	28. C	29. A	30. C

國家圖書館出版品預行編目資料

全民英檢聽力測驗 SO EASY (初級篇)／三民英語編
輯小組彙整.——三版三刷.——臺北市：三民，2024
　　面；　公分

　　ISBN 978-957-14-7139-6 （平裝）
　　1. 英語 2. 問題集

805.1892　　　　　　　　　　　　110000641

全民英檢聽力測驗 SO EASY (初級篇)

彙　　　整	三民英語編輯小組
內頁繪圖	吳玫青　霸　子

創 辦 人	劉振強
發 行 人	劉仲傑
出 版 者	三民書局股份有限公司 (成立於 1953 年)

三民網路書店
https://www.sanmin.com.tw

地　　　址	臺北市復興北路 386 號	(復北門市)	(02)2500-6600
	臺北市重慶南路一段 61 號	(重南門市)	(02)2361-7511

出版日期	初版一刷 2007 年 8 月
	三版一刷 2021 年 3 月
	三版三刷 2024 年 7 月
書籍編號	S807070
I S B N	978-957-14-7139-6

全民英檢
聽力測驗
SO EASY

初級篇

三版

三民英語編輯小組　彙整

最新穎！符合全新改版英檢題型
最逼真！模擬試題提升應試能力
最精闢！範例分析傾授高分技巧

解答本

三民書局

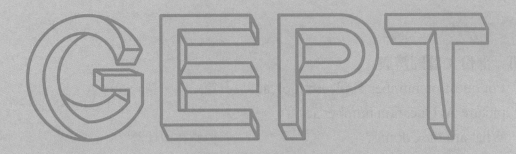

聽力測驗
腳本與解答

第一部份：看圖辨義

1. For question number 1, please look at picture A. Question number 1:

   What are they doing?

   (A) They are wearing suits.

   (B) They are shaking hands.

   (C) They are waving hands.

   第一題，請看圖片 A。第一題：

   他們在做什麼？

   選項：(A) 他們正在穿套裝。

   　　　(B) 他們正在握手。

   　　　(C) 他們正在揮手。

   答案 B

2. For questions number 2 and 3, please look at picture B. Question number 2:

   What information is given in this form?

   (A) The books Bob likes to read.

   (B) The activities Bob likes to do.

   (C) The company Bob works for.

   第二題及第三題，請看圖片 B。第二題：

   表單中提供了什麼資訊？

   選項：(A) 鮑伯喜歡閱讀的書。

   　　　(B) 鮑伯喜歡做的活動。

   　　　(C) 鮑伯工作的公司。

   答案 B

3. Question number 3, please look at picture B again.

   Who might read this form?

   (A) A teacher.

   (B) A doctor.

   (C) A driver.

   第三題，請再看一次圖片 B。

   誰可能會看這個表單？

   選項：(A) 一位老師。

   　　　(B) 一位醫生。

   　　　(C) 一位司機。

   答案 A

4. For question number 4, please look at picture C. Question number 4:

   What does this map tell us?

   (A) Go straight and turn right.

   (B) Go straight and turn left.

   (C) Go straight for two blocks.

   第四題，請看圖片 C。第四題：

   這張地圖告訴我們什麼？

   選項：(A) 直走然後右轉。

   　　　(B) 直走然後左轉。

   　　　(C) 往前直走兩個街區。

   答案 C

5. For question number 5, please look at

   第五題，請看圖片 D。第五題：

picture D. Question number 5:

What would you say about this woman?

(A) She changes her hairstyle.

(B) She is thinner than before.

(C) She wears new glasses.

答案 **B**

你會如何形容這女生？

選項：(A) 她改變了她的髮型。

(B) 她比以前瘦。

(C) 她戴了新的眼鏡。

第二部份：問答

6. I haven't seen you for weeks. How are you doing?

(A) Thanks a lot.

(B) I am reading.

(C) Couldn't be better.

答案 **C**

好幾週沒見到你了。你好嗎？

選項：(A) 非常感謝。

(B) 我正在閱讀。

(C) 再好不過了。

7. What do you like to do in your free time?

(A) I went to a movie last night.

(B) I play basketball and listen to music.

(C) Can you give me a few minutes?

答案 **B**

你在空閒時間喜歡做什麼？

選項：(A) 我昨晚去看了一場電影。

(B) 我會打籃球和聽音樂。

(C) 你能給我幾分鐘時間嗎？

8. Do you know where the ABC Bank is?

(A) It's on my table.

(B) No, the river bank is ugly.

(C) I'm sorry. I don't know where it is.

答案 **C**

你知道 ABC 銀行在哪裡嗎？

選項：(A) 它在我的桌上。

(B) 不，那河岸很醜。

(C) 抱歉。我不知道在哪裡。

9. How long will it take to have my phone fixed?

(A) It's a long story.

(B) It's about time.

(C) About a week.

答案 **C**

我的手機需要多久才能修理好？

選項：(A) 說來話長。

(B) 早該如此。

(C) 約一個星期。

10. Could you do me a favor?

(A) Sure. This is my favorite.

你能幫我一個忙嗎？

選項：(A) 當然。這是我最喜愛的。

(B) Of course. What is it?

(C) Yes, I think I have a fever.

11. Sorry, there are no tables available tonight.

(A) Tonight is a beautiful night.

(B) I like the tables very much.

(C) Well, how about tomorrow?

12. They're showing a new movie on Saturday. Are you interested?

(A) Today is Sunday.

(B) I'll be glad to help.

(C) Sure, let's go see it.

13. I really appreciate your help.

(A) Sure, she will help.

(B) It's no big deal.

(C) No, I can't.

14. Sir, could you give me another day to finish my report?

(A) All right. Just make sure it won't happen again.

(B) Sure. It is the best report that I have ever read.

(C) Thanks. I'll finish it on time.

15. Simon, please answer this question.

(A) Sure, Mr. Smith.

(B) I'm sorry. I lost it.

(C) Nothing much.

(B) 當然。是什麼事？

(C) 是的，我想我發燒了。

抱歉，今天晚上已經客滿了。

選項：(A) 今晚是個美麗的夜晚。

(B) 我非常喜歡這些桌子。

(C) 那麼明天呢？

星期六有一部新的電影上映。你有興趣嗎？

選項：(A) 今天是星期日。

(B) 我很樂意幫忙。

(C) 好啊，我們去看。

我真的很感激你的幫忙。

選項：(A) 當然，她會幫忙。

(B) 這沒什麼。

(C) 不，我不行。

老師，你能再給我一天的時間來完成報告嗎？

選項：(A) 好吧。只要你切記下不為例。

(B) 當然。這是我讀過最棒的報告。

(C) 謝謝。我會準時完成。

賽門，請回答這一題。

選項：(A) 好的，史密斯老師。

(B) 很抱歉。我弄丟了。

(C) 沒什麼事。

第三部份：簡短對話

16. W: David! It's been a long time. How's everything?

    M: Just fine. I've been to London for two weeks.

    W: Really? That sounds great.

    M: Well, actually, I was there on business.

    Q: Who are the speakers?

    　(A) They work together and see each other every day.

    　(B) They don't know each other.

    　(C) They are friends, but they haven't seen each other a while ago.

女：大衛！好久不見了。你過得如何？

男：還不錯。我去了倫敦兩週。

女：真的嗎？聽起來很棒。

男：嗯…其實，我是去那裡出差。

問題：說話者是什麼人？

選項：(A) 他們一起工作而且天天見面。

　　　(B) 他們不認識對方。

　　　(C) 他們是朋友，不過已經很久沒見面了。

17. W: Ken, what do you do in your free time?

    M: Oh, I play basketball whenever I can.

    W: I like to play basketball, too. Why don't we play it together next time?

    M: Sure. That would be nice!

    Q: What does Ken do when he is free?

    　(A) He plays instruments.

    　(B) He plays sports.

    　(C) He plays video games.

女：肯，你空閒的時候都做什麼？

男：喔，我只要一有時間就打籃球。

女：我也喜歡打籃球。要不要下次一起打？

男：當然。那真是太好了！

問題：肯空閒的時候都做什麼？

選項：(A) 他彈奏樂器。

　　　(B) 他從事運動。

　　　(C) 他打電動遊戲。

18. M: Excuse me. Can you tell me where the King's Restaurant is?

    W: Go straight for three blocks and turn left. It will be on your right-hand side.

    M: Can you draw me a map?

    W: Yes, of course.

男：不好意思。你能告訴我國王餐廳在哪裡嗎？

女：直走三個街區再左轉。它會在你的右手邊。

男：你可以幫我畫張地圖嗎？

女：當然可以。

Q: Where does the man want to go? 問題：這男生想要去哪裡？
   (A) A restroom. 選項：(A) 一間洗手間。
   (B) A block.   (B) 一個街區。
   (C) A restaurant.   (C) 一間餐廳。

答案 **C**

19. M: Hello. May I speak to Mr. Wu, please? 男：喂。我可以跟吳先生講話嗎？

W: I'm sorry. He's in a meeting right now. May I ask who's calling? 女：很抱歉。他正在開會。請問你是哪位呢？

M: Jack. I'm a teacher from San Min Elementary School. 男：傑克。我是三民國小的老師。

W: I see. Would you like to leave a message? 女：我知道了。你要留話嗎？

M: That's OK. I'll try again later. Thank you. 男：沒關係。我等一下再撥。謝謝你。

Q: Why couldn't Mr. Wu answer the phone? 問題：為什麼吳先生不能接電話？

   (A) He's talking to Jack. 選項：(A) 他正在和傑克講電話。
   (B) He's out for lunch.   (B) 他出去吃午餐。
   (C) He's in a meeting.   (C) 他正在開會。

答案 **C**

20. W: I'd like to see Mr. Lee sometime this week. 女：我想在這星期找一個時間跟李先生見面。

M: Sure, how about Friday afternoon? 男：好，星期五下午如何？

W: That'd be great. What time? 女：非常好。什麼時候？

M: He will be busy from 1 to 2 p.m. How about 3 p.m.? 男：他下午一點到兩點會很忙碌。下午三點呢？

W: Sure. No problem. 女：好。沒問題。

Q: When will the woman see Mr. Lee? 問題：這女生何時要跟李先生見面？

   (A) Wednesday at 2:00 p.m. 選項：(A) 星期三下午兩點。
   (B) Thursday at 1:00 p.m.   (B) 星期四下午一點。
   (C) Friday at 3:00 p.m.   (C) 星期五下午三點。

答案 **C**

21. W: I'm having a party at my apartment next Friday. Would you like to come?

M: Sure. What kind of party are you having?

W: Actually, it's my birthday.

Q: What kind of party is the woman having?

   (A) A party for her new apartment.

   (B) A party for her birthday.

   (C) A party for her new job.

答案 **B**

女：下星期五我將在我的公寓辦一個派對。你願意來嗎？

男：當然。你要辦什麼樣的派對？

女：事實上，那天是我的生日。

問題：這女生將要辦什麼樣的派對？

選項：(A) 慶祝搬到新公寓的派對。

     (B) 慶祝她生日的派對。

     (C) 慶祝她新工作的派對。

22. W: Mike, could you pick up Karen for me at the train station?

M: Sure, when will she arrive?

W: 6 p.m. After picking up Karen, can you go to the market for me?

M: OK. What do you need?

W: Three oranges.

Q: What will the man most likely do next?

   (A) Buy some fruit.

   (B) Go to the train station.

   (C) Give Karen a call.

答案 **B**

女：麥克，你能幫我到火車站去接凱倫嗎？

男：當然，她什麼時候到？

女：晚上六點。接完凱倫，你可以幫我跑一趟市場嗎？

男：好。你需要什麼？

女：三顆橘子。

問題：這男生接下來最有可能做什麼？

選項：(A) 買一些水果。

     (B) 去火車站。

     (C) 打給凱倫。

23. W: Jerry, have you finished your homework?

M: No, I haven't started it yet.

W: Why?

M: I was too sleepy last night and I fell asleep.

W: You must hurry up or you can't hand it in today.

女：傑瑞，你完成你的家庭作業了嗎？

男：還沒，我還沒開始寫。

女：為什麼？

男：我昨晚太想睡，然後就睡著了。

女：你必須趕快，否則無法在今天繳交作業。

Q: Why has Jerry NOT finished his homework?

    (A) He didn't know how to do it.

    (B) He was too tired to do it.

    (C) He forgot to hand it in.

問題：為什麼傑瑞還沒有完成他的家庭作業？

選項：(A) 他不知道該怎麼做。

    (B) 他太累而無法做作業。

    (C) 他忘了交作業。

答案　B

24. M: I think it's fun to swing the bat and run.

    W: So do I. But I've broken the window when hitting the ball.

    M: Really? Then what happened?

    W: My parents didn't blame me. They found someone to fix it.

    Q: Which sport are they most likely talking about?

        (A) Tennis.

        (B) Baseball.

        (C) Basketball.

男：我覺得揮棒和跑壘很有意思。

女：我也是。但我曾經在擊球時打破窗戶。

男：真的嗎？接著發生什麼事？

女：我父母沒有罵我。他們找人來修理。

問題：他們最有可能在討論什麼運動？

選項：(A) 網球。

    (B) 棒球。

    (C) 籃球。

答案　B

25. W: Arthur, now I know why you like this hotel so much.

    M: All the people working here are really nice to the guests.

    W: Yes. I'll tell my friends to stay here when they come to the city.

    Q: What does the man like about this hotel?

        (A) Its service.

        (B) Its rooms.

        (C) Its food.

女：亞瑟，我現在知道你為什麼這麼喜歡這間飯店了。

男：這裡所有的工作人員都真的對客人很好。

女：是的。我會告訴我朋友，當他們來這個城市時，一定要住這裡。

問題：這男生喜歡這間飯店的哪一點？

選項：(A) 它的服務。

    (B) 它的房間。

    (C) 它的食物。

答案　A

第四部份：短文聽解

26. For question number 26, please look at the three pictures. Question number 26, listen to the following announcement. Where will Miss Chen go?

Your attention please. A lost girl, Susan, was found at the ticket office, and she was looking for her mother, Ms. Lucy Chen. Ms. Chen, please come to the information center on the first floor. Your daughter is waiting for you. Thank you.

(A) The information desk.

(B) The cash desk.

(C) The ticket office.

第二十六題，請看這三張圖。第二十六題，注意聆聽接下來的廣播。陳小姐將會去哪裡？

請注意。我們在售票處找到一位走失的女生——蘇珊，她在尋找她的母親——陳露西女士。陳女士，請到一樓的服務櫃臺，你的女兒正在等你。謝謝你。

選項：(A) 服務櫃臺。

(B) 結帳櫃臺。

(C) 售票處。

答案 **A**

27. For question number 27, please look at the three pictures. Question number 27, listen to the following announcement. Where will you most probably hear this announcement?

Good morning, all passengers. Welcome aboard train 1009. Our destination is Kaohsiung, and this train will stop at Taipei, Taoyuan, Hsinchu, Miaoli, Taichung, Changhua, Chiayi, Tainan and Kaohsiung. Have a nice trip.

(A) At the airport.

(B) On the train.

(C) At the bus station.

第二十七題，請看這三張圖。第二十七題，注意聆聽接下來的廣播。你最有可能在哪裡聽到這則廣播？

各位乘客早安。歡迎搭乘 1009 號列車。我們的終點站是高雄，本列車將停靠臺北、桃園、新竹、苗栗、臺中、彰化、嘉義、臺南和高雄。祝您旅途愉快。

選項：(A) 在機場。

(B) 在火車上。

(C) 在公車站。

答案 **B**

28. For question number 28, please look at the three pictures. Question number 28,

第二十八題，請看這三張圖。第二十八題，一位男生正在留語音訊息給泰

a man is leaving a phone message for Ted. What will be returned to Ted tomorrow?

Ted, I put the book you lent me last month on the bookshelf. I'm sorry I forgot to bring the Elton John's album with me today. I will give it back to you tomorrow. I promise.

(A) A bookshelf.

(B) An album.

(C) A book.

德。明天什麼東西將被歸還給泰德？

泰德，我把你上個月借給我的書放在書櫃裡。很抱歉我今天忘了帶艾爾頓·約翰的專輯。我明天會把它還給你，我保證。

選項：(A) 一個書櫃。

　　　(B) 一張專輯。

　　　(C) 一本書。

答案 **B**

29. For question number 29, please look at the three pictures. Question number 29, listen to the following short talk. What will Mr. Lin most probably do on May 8th?

Mr. Lin, you have booked a seat on flight CX812, leaving at 7:30 a.m. on May 10th. It arrives in Hong Kong at 9:20 a.m., and your computer code is CA1234. Please call back on May 8th to confirm your reservation with it. Thanks.

(A) Play video games.

(B) Use a computer.

(C) Make a phone call.

第二十九題，請看這三張圖。第二十九題，注意聆聽接下來的簡短談話。林先生在五月八日時最有可能做什麼？

林先生，您已預訂 CX812 班機的座位，起飛時間為五月十日上午七點三十分。上午九點二十分抵達香港。您的電腦代號為 CA1234。請在五月八日來電以此電腦代號確認您的訂位。謝謝。

選項：(A) 玩電動。

　　　(B) 用電腦。

　　　(C) 打電話。

答案 **C**

30. For question number 30, please look at the three pictures. Question number 30, Carla is talking about her dog. Where will Carla go this weekend?

My dog looks sick. It becomes thinner and doesn't eat anything. Also, it sleeps

第三十題，請看這三張圖。第三十題，卡拉正在談論她的狗。卡拉這個週末去哪裡？

我的狗看起來生病了。牠越來越瘦，而且什麼都不吃。牠也整天都在睡覺，

all day and is no longer full of energy. I'm worried about it. My mother suggests that I take my dog to the vet this weekend.

(A) A park.

(B) An animal hospital.

(C) A beach.

答案 **B**

不再充滿活力。我很擔心牠。我的母親建議我週末時把狗帶去看獸醫。

選項：(A) 公園。

(B) 動物醫院。

(C) 海邊。

第一部份：看圖辨義

1. For question number 1, please look at picture A. Question number 1:

    Why does the man feel sorry?

    (A) They are old friends.

    (B) Her name is Mary.

    (C) He has the wrong number.

    答案　**C**

    第一題，請看圖片 A。第一題：

    為什麼這男生覺得抱歉？

    選項：(A) 他們是老朋友。

    　　　(B) 她名叫瑪莉。

    　　　(C) 他撥錯電話號碼。

2. For questions number 2 and 3, please look at picture B. Question number 2:

    How does the woman feel about the music?

    (A) She can't stand it.

    (B) She enjoys it very much.

    (C) She is crazy about it.

    答案　**A**

    第二題及第三題，請看圖片 B。第二題：

    這女生對這音樂的感覺如何？

    選項：(A) 她無法忍受。

    　　　(B) 她非常樂在其中。

    　　　(C) 她瘋狂喜歡這音樂。

3. Question number 3, please look at picture B again. What is the woman most likely saying to the man?

    (A) May I borrow your album?

    (B) Can you turn down the music?

    (C) The CD player is broken.

    答案　**B**

    第三題，請再看一次圖片 B。這女生最有可能對這男生說什麼？

    選項：(A) 我可以跟你借專輯嗎？

    　　　(B) 你可以把音樂轉小聲嗎？

    　　　(C) CD 播放器壞掉了。

4. For question number 4, please look at picture C. Question number 4:

    What did the man do to the old lady?

    (A) He helped her cross the road.

    (B) He gave her some money.

    (C) He invited her to dinner.

    答案　**A**

    第四題，請看圖片 C。第四題：

    這男生對這位老太太做了什麼？

    選項：(A) 他幫助她過馬路。

    　　　(B) 他給了她一些錢。

    　　　(C) 他邀請她吃晚餐。

5. For question number 5, please look at picture D. Question number 5:

What subject is this teacher teaching?

(A) Math.

(B) English.

(C) Geography.

答案　**C**

第五題，請看圖片 D。第五題：

這老師教的是什麼科目？

選項：(A) 數學。

(B) 英文。

(C) 地理。

第二部份：問答

6. How have you been doing these days?

(A) Wonderful.

(B) He is doing it now.

(C) I'm a student.

答案　**A**

你最近這一陣子好嗎？

選項：(A) 很好。

(B) 他正在做。

(C) 我是一個學生。

7. What's your favorite subject at school?

(A) English.

(B) Video games.

(C) French fries.

答案　**A**

你在學校最喜歡的科目是什麼？

選項：(A) 英文。

(B) 電動遊戲。

(C) 炸薯條。

8. Do you know where I can find a post office?

(A) No. The bank opens at 9:00 a.m.

(B) Sure. Walk straight and you'll see it on your right.

(C) It'll be the best way to get there.

答案　**B**

你知道我可以在哪裡找到郵局嗎？

選項：(A) 不。銀行早上九點開門。

(B) 當然。直走然後你就會看到在右手邊。

(C) 這是到那邊的最好方法。

9. Why don't you go with us?

(A) I have homework to do.

(B) I prefer this bag to that one.

(C) I walk home after school.

答案　**A**

你為什麼不跟我們一起去？

選項：(A) 我有作業要寫。

(B) 跟那個袋子比，我比較喜歡這個。

(C) 我放學走路回家。

10. I was wondering if I could borrow your motorcycle.

    (A) It's none of your business.

    (B) Your bicycle is wonderful.

    (C) No problem.

我想請問一下能不能借用你的機車。

選項：(A) 這不關你的事。

(B) 你的腳踏車棒極了。

(C) 沒問題。

答案 C

11. How about tomorrow afternoon at 2 o'clock?

    (A) OK. I'll be there.

    (B) No, tomorrow will be fine.

    (C) Sure. What time?

明天下午兩點如何？

選項：(A) 沒問題。我會到場。

(B) 不，明天蠻適合的。

(C) 當然。什麼時候？

答案 A

12. I can give you a ride to the mall.

    (A) It was a good ride.

    (B) That would be great!

    (C) I think I'm right about it.

我可以載你一程到購物中心。

選項：(A) 那是一段美好的旅程。

(B) 那太好了！

(C) 我想我是對的。

答案 B

13. Thanks for letting me use your cell phone.

    (A) Sure. Anytime.

    (B) Sure. Here you go.

    (C) Sure. Give me a call.

謝謝你讓我使用你的手機。

選項：(A) 沒什麼。隨時歡迎。

(B) 沒什麼。拿去吧。

(C) 沒什麼。打電話給我。

答案 A

14. Excuse me. Could you keep your voice down? This is a library.

    (A) Sure. Which book?

    (B) Oh, I'm sorry.

    (C) Yes, I have a voice mailbox.

不好意思。你可以把你的音量降低嗎？這是一所圖書館。

選項：(A) 當然。哪一本書？

(B) 噢，我很抱歉。

(C) 是的，我有一個語音信箱。

答案 B

15. Can I take a look at the menu? Thank you.

    (A) Fine, thank you, and you?

我可以看一下菜單嗎？謝謝。

選項：(A) 很好，謝謝你，那你呢？

(B) No problem. Here you go.

(C) How's everything today?

(B) 沒問題。這是你要的菜單。

(C) 今天過得如何？

答案 **B**

第三部份：簡短對話

16. W: What's wrong with you? You look pale.

    M: I think I caught a cold.

    W: You'd better go to see a doctor.

    M: It's no big deal. I'll recover soon after taking a rest.

    Q: What will the man most likely do next?

    (A) Go to a hospital.

    (B) Make a deal.

    (C) Go to bed.

女：你怎麼了？你看起來很蒼白。

男：我覺得我感冒了。

女：你最好去看醫生。

男：沒什麼大不了的。我休息後很快就會恢復。

問題：這男生接下來最有可能做什麼？

選項：(A) 去醫院。

(B) 做交易。

(C) 上床睡覺。

答案 **C**

17. W: David, are you the only child in your family?

    M: No, I have a brother and two sisters.

    W: Wow, that's a lot. Does your grandpa live with you?

    M: I only live with my brother, sisters and parents.

    Q: How many family members does David live with?

    (A) Three.

    (B) Four.

    (C) Five.

女：大衛，你是家裡唯一的小孩嗎？

男：不是，我有一個兄弟和兩個姊妹。

女：哇，你有好多兄弟姊妹。你爺爺跟你住在一起嗎？

男：我只和兄弟、姊妹及父母一起住。

問題：大衛和幾個家庭成員住在一起？

選項：(A) 三個。

(B) 四個。

(C) 五個。

答案 **C**

18. M: Hi, Janet. Where are you headed?

    W: I am going to Taipei.

男：嗨，珍妮。你要去哪裡？

女：我要去臺北。

M: Taipei? But the train from this platform heads south. You should go to platform 3.

W: Oh, I didn't notice that. I'd better hurry up! Thank you.

Q: Where are the speakers?

    (A) At a train station.

    (B) In Taipei.

    (C) At a bus stop.

男：臺北?但這個月臺的列車是往南。你應該去第三月臺。

女：哦，我沒注意到。我最好加快腳步了！謝謝你。

問題：說話者在什麼地方？

選項：(A) 在火車站。

    (B) 在臺北。

    (C) 在公車站。

答案 **A**

19. W: Can you do me a favor?

M: Sure. What is it?

W: My sister is coming from Taichung tomorrow. Could you pick her up at the train station?

M: OK. What time will she arrive?

Q: Who is going to pick up the woman's sister?

    (A) The woman.

    (B) The woman's sister.

    (C) The man.

女：可以請你幫個忙嗎？

男：當然。是什麼？

女：我妹妹明天要從臺中過來。你能到火車站接她嗎？

男：好。她什麼時候到？

問題：誰將要去接這女生的妹妹？

選項：(A) 這女生。

    (B) 這女生的妹妹。

    (C) 這男生。

答案 **C**

20. W: Hi, I'd like to see Dr. Kitty because I have terrible toothache.

M: When would you like to see her?

W: Oh, will tomorrow afternoon be fine?

M: Well, how about 2:30?

W: That'll be great. Thank you.

Q: Why does the woman want to see Dr. Kitty?

    (A) She has a fever.

    (B) Her leg is broken.

女：嗨，我想見凱蒂醫生，因為我的牙痛得很嚴重。

男：你想要什麼時候見她？

女：喔，明天下午可以嗎？

男：嗯，兩點半如何？

女：那樣很好。謝謝你。

問題：為什麼這女生想見凱蒂醫生？

選項：(A) 她發燒了。

    (B) 她的腿斷掉了。

(C) She has a pain in a tooth.

(C) 她的牙齒痛。

答案 C

21. M: Are you free later today?

男：你今天等一下有空嗎？

W: Maybe. Why?

女：也許吧。什麼事？

M: There's a new ice cream store in town. Would you like to try?

男：城裡有一家新的冰淇淋店。你想不想試試看？

W: That'd be great. Give me a couple of minutes to finish my report.

女：好啊。給我兩分鐘完成我的報告。

Q: What will the man and woman do later that day?

問題：那天稍晚的時候這男生和女生將要做什麼？

(A) They're going to finish a report together.

選項：(A) 他們將要一起完成一份報告。

(B) They're going to have some desserts.

(B) 他們將要去吃甜點。

(C) They're going to a movie.

(C) 他們將要去看電影。

答案 B

22. W: Hey, I bought you a little something.

女：嘿，我買了一個小東西給你。

M: Oh, you shouldn't have. Can I open it?

男：噢，你不必這樣啦。我可以打開嗎？

W: Sure. Go ahead.

女：當然。請便。

M: Oh, it's so nice. How did you know I need a new watch?

男：噢，太好了。你怎麼知道我需要一只新手錶？

Q: What did the woman do?

問題：這女生做了什麼？

(A) She fixed the watch for the man.

選項：(A) 她幫這男生修好了手錶。

(B) She lent her watch to the man.

(B) 她把她的錶借給這男生。

(C) She bought a watch for the man.

(C) 她買了一只錶給這男生。

答案 C

23. M: Sharon, you don't look good. What's wrong?

男：莎朗，你看起來不太好。怎麼了？

W: Oh, I didn't sleep well last night. My neighbor's dog was barking all night long.

女：喔，我昨天晚上沒睡好。我鄰居的狗整個晚上叫個不停。

M: Me, too. I couldn't sleep last night. Schoolwork stresses me out.

W: That's awful. You should relax more.

Q: What did Sharon complain about?

    (A) Schoolwork.

    (B) Noise.

    (C) Sports.

男：我也是，我昨晚睡不著。學校課業讓我焦慮不安。

女：太糟糕了。你應該放鬆一點。

問題：莎朗在抱怨什麼？

選項：(A) 學校課業。

    (B) 噪音。

    (C) 運動。

答案 B

24. M: I hear there'll be a football game against Eastern High.

W: Really? When?

M: Next Saturday. Would you like to come with me?

W: Sure. I hope our school beats them.

Q: What will these people do next Saturday?

    (A) Play football.

    (B) Play video games.

    (C) Watch a game.

男：我聽說將會有一場對抗東區高中的美式足球賽。

女：真的嗎？什麼時候？

男：下一個星期六。你想要跟我一起去嗎？

女：當然。我希望我們的校隊能打敗他們。

問題：下星期六說話者要做什麼？

選項：(A) 踢美式足球。

    (B) 打電動遊戲。

    (C) 看一場比賽。

答案 C

25. M: Um, Melody, you're right. The steak here is delicious.

W: I knew you would like it. Wait until you try their desserts.

M: Are they good, too? I can hardly wait to have some.

Q: What does the woman like about this restaurant?

    (A) Its prices.

    (B) Its food.

    (C) Its service.

男：嗯，美樂蒂，你說得沒錯。這裡的牛排很美味。

女：我就知道你會喜歡。等一下你再試試看他們的甜點。

男：它們也很讚嗎？我真等不及想要來一點。

問題：這女生喜歡這家餐廳的哪一點？

選項：(A) 它的價位。

    (B) 它的食物。

    (C) 它的服務。

第四部份：短文聽解

26. For question number 26, please look at the three pictures. Question number 26, listen to the following announcement. What is on sale?

Ladies and gentlemen, welcome to San Min Department Store. Today only! Hats for only NT$200. Buy two, get one free! This is a once-in-a-lifetime chance. Don't miss it and enjoy your shopping.

(A) Pants.

(B) Hats.

(C) Shoes.

第二十六題，請看這三張圖。第二十六題，注意聆聽接下來的廣播。什麼東西正在特賣？

各位先生女士們，歡迎來到三民百貨公司。只有在今天哦！帽子只要兩百元。買二送一！這是一生一次的機會。千萬別錯過它，祝您購物愉快。

選項：(A) 褲子。

(B) 帽子。

(C) 鞋子。

27. For question number 27, please look at the three pictures. Question number 27, Roger is leaving a phone message for Kevin. Why can't Roger be on time?

Hey, Kevin. This is Roger. I'm just calling to let you know that I'll be a little late to the party. I'm working overtime to get things done. And I'll buy some food for the party. See you then.

(A) He is working.

(B) He is sleeping.

(C) He is eating his dinner.

第二十七題，請看這三張圖。第二十七題，羅傑正在留語音訊息給凱文。為什麼羅傑無法準時到？

嘿！凱文，我是羅傑。我打來是要讓你知道我會晚一點到派對上。我要加班把事情做完，還有我會買一些食物到派對去。到時見。

選項：(A) 他在工作。

(B) 他在睡覺。

(C) 他在吃晚餐。

28. For question number 28, please look at the three pictures. Question number 28, listen to the following message for

第二十八題，請看這三張圖。第二十八題，注意聆聽接下來給蕾貝卡的留言。蕾貝卡最有可能買什麼？

Rebecca. What will Rebecca most probably buy?

Rebecca, this is Mom. This morning I found that we were running out of milk. Would you please buy a bottle of milk at the supermarket on your way home? Thank you. Oh, by the way, I have a meeting tonight, so I won't be home till 11. I'll bring you your favorite cheesecake. Bye.

(A) Bread.

(B) Milk.

(C) Cheesecake.

蕾貝卡，我是媽媽。我今天早上發現我們沒有牛奶了。可不可以請你在回家的路上到超市去買一瓶牛奶回來？謝謝你。哦，對了，我今晚有個會議，所以十一點以前不會在家。我會帶你最愛的起司蛋糕給你。再見。

選項：(A) 麵包。

　　　(B) 牛奶。

　　　(C) 起司蛋糕。

答案 B

29. For question number 29, please look at the three pictures. Question number 29, Peter is talking about his future plan. What will Peter most probably buy?

I'm going to college in September. I plan to rent an apartment near my school. Also, I want to buy a notebook instead of a desktop computer because it will be more convenient for me to bring it to school.

(A) A notebook.

(B) A desktop computer.

(C) An apartment.

第二十九題，請看這三張圖。第二十九題，彼得正在談論他未來的計畫。彼得最有可能買什麼？

我將在九月時去上大學。我打算在學校附近租一間公寓。另外，我想要買一臺筆記型電腦，而不是桌上型電腦，因為帶它去學校時比較方便。

選項：(A) 筆記型電腦。

　　　(B) 桌上型電腦。

　　　(C) 一間公寓。

答案 A

30. For question number 30, please look at the three pictures. Question number 30, listen to the following announcement. Where will you most probably hear this

第三十題，請看這三張圖。第三十題，注意聆聽接下來的廣播。你最有可能在哪裡聽到這則廣播？

20

announcement?

Your attention please. This is an emergency! There is a fire in the kitchen. I repeat, there is a fire in the kitchen. Please leave this building immediately by the nearest emergency exit. Please walk, and do not panic.

(A) In a movie theater.

(B) In a restaurant.

(C) In a store.

答案 **B**

請注意！這是緊急事件！廚房發生火警。重覆一次，廚房發生火警。請盡速由最近的緊急逃生口離開這棟大樓。請用走的，並且請不要驚慌。

選項：(A) 電影院裡。

(B) 餐廳裡。

(C) 賣場裡。

第一部份：看圖辨義

1. For question number 1, please look at picture A. Question number 1:

   Where is the boy?

   (A) He is catching a fish.

   (B) He is standing by a river.

   (C) He is on the top of a mountain.

   第一題，請看圖片 A。第一題：

   這男孩在哪裡？

   選項：(A) 他正在抓一條魚。

   (B) 他站在河邊。

   (C) 他在山頂上。

   答案 **B**

2. For questions number 2 and 3, please look at picture B. Question number 2:

   Where is this little boy?

   (A) He's in the forest.

   (B) He's in the museum.

   (C) He's in the zoo.

   第二題及第三題，請看圖片 B。第二題：

   這小男孩在哪裡？

   選項：(A) 他在森林裡。

   (B) 他在博物館裡。

   (C) 他在動物園裡。

   答案 **C**

3. Question number 3, please look at picture B again. What does this sign tell visitors?

   (A) It's a tiger.

   (B) Be careful.

   (C) Do not take photos.

   第三題，請再看一次圖片 B。這個告示告訴遊客什麼？

   選項：(A) 牠是一隻老虎。

   (B) 要小心。

   (C) 禁止拍照。

   答案 **B**

4. For question number 4, please look at picture C. Question number 4:

   What is the woman most likely saying to the man?

   (A) It's okay. Never mind.

   (B) Why do you look so happy?

   (C) I'm sorry. I'll never do it again.

   第四題，請看圖片 C。第四題：

   這女生最有可能對這男生說什麼？

   選項：(A) 沒事，別放在心上。

   (B) 你為何看起來那麼開心？

   (C) 抱歉。我不會再這麼做。

   答案 **A**

5. For question number 5, please look at

   第五題，請看圖片 D。第五題：

picture D. Question number 5:

What are they doing?

(A) They are holding a ball.

(B) They are playing basketball.

(C) They are running.

他們在做什麼？

選項：(A) 他們正在拿著一顆球。

(B) 他們正在打籃球。

(C) 他們正在跑步。

答案 **B**

第二部份：問答

6. How's it going?

(A) It's 9:00 now.

(B) OK, I guess.

(C) It's going to rain.

一切可好？

選項：(A) 現在九點了。

(B) 我想還可以啦。

(C) 快要下雨了。

答案 **B**

7. What does your father do?

(A) He is fine. Thanks.

(B) He is fixing my bike for me.

(C) He's a police officer.

你父親是做什麼工作？

選項：(A) 他很好。謝謝。

(B) 他正在幫我修理腳踏車。

(C) 他是一個警員。

答案 **C**

8. Could you tell me how to get to the MRT station?

(A) Yes. Thank you very much.

(B) The next bus stop is 500 meters away.

(C) Go straight. It's only two blocks down the road.

你可以告訴我如何到捷運站嗎？

選項：(A) 是的。非常感謝。

(B) 下一個公車站牌在五百公尺外。

(C) 直走過去。它就在這條路上，只有兩個街區遠。

答案 **C**

9. Do you want to leave a message?

(A) Hold on. Let me get her for you.

(B) Sure. I'll call her back.

(C) Yes. Could you ask her to call Tom?

你要留言嗎？

選項：(A) 請等一下。我幫你去叫她。

(B) 當然。我會再打給她。

(C) 好。你能請她打電話給湯姆嗎？

答案 **C**

10. Would you help me move this box?
    (A) Yes. Go ahead.
    (B) Sure, no problem.
    (C) No, thank you.

    答案 **B**

你能幫我搬這個箱子嗎？
選項：(A) 是的。去做吧。
      (B) 當然，沒問題。
      (C) 不，謝了。

11. How did you like my cooking tonight?
    (A) I don't feel like cooking.
    (B) I like cooking very much.
    (C) It was really delicious.

    答案 **C**

你覺得我今晚的廚藝如何？
選項：(A) 我不喜歡下廚。
      (B) 我非常喜歡烹飪。
      (C) 真的非常美味。

12. Would you like a little more salad?
    (A) No, thank you.
    (B) I'll call you later.
    (C) You are welcome.

    答案 **A**

你還想要再來一些沙拉嗎？
選項：(A) 不，謝謝你。
      (B) 我晚一點打電話給你。
      (C) 不客氣。

13. Thank you for such a wonderful dinner.
    (A) Sounds great. I'll go, too.
    (B) I'll be there for dinner.
    (C) My pleasure.

    答案 **C**

謝謝你招待我這麼棒的晚餐。
選項：(A) 聽起來不錯。我也要去。
      (B) 我會過去吃晚餐。
      (C) 這是我的榮幸。

14. Alice, I heard you're crazy about fishing.
    (A) Fish is not my favorite food.
    (B) That's right. I like fishing very much.
    (C) Fishing is not crazy at all.

    答案 **B**

愛麗絲，我聽說你很喜歡釣魚。
選項：(A) 魚不是我最喜歡的食物。
      (B) 沒錯。我非常喜歡釣魚。
      (C) 釣魚一點也不瘋狂。

15. I'm sorry, Ms. Wang. I don't know the answer to that question.
    (A) I'm glad you asked.
    (B) Where is my answering machine?
    (C) Well, you'd better study harder.

    答案 **C**

很抱歉，王老師。我不知道那個問題的答案。
選項：(A) 很高興你這樣問。
      (B) 我的電話答錄機在哪裡？
      (C) 嗯，你要再用功一點。

第三部份：簡短對話

16. M: Hey, would you like to have some cakes? They are delicious!

    W: Oh, no. Sorry, I'm on a diet.

    M: Come on. Just have a bite.

    W: Thanks, but I've made up my mind.

    Q: What does the woman plan to do?

    　(A) Think something in her mind.

    　(B) Eat a slice of cake.

    　(C) Lose some weight.

男：嘿，你想吃一些蛋糕嗎？它們很好吃喔！

女：哦，不了。抱歉，我在減肥。

男：快點，吃一口就好。

女：謝謝，但是我已經下定決心了。

問題：這女生計畫做什麼？

選項：(A) 在心裡想事情。

　　　(B) 吃一片蛋糕。

　　　(C) 減重。

答案 C

17. W: Could you please give me a glass of juice?

    M: Sure, anything else?

    W: I think I'll have steak and some fries.

    M: OK. Would you like to have a dessert?

    W: No, that will be all, thank you.

    Q: How many things does the woman order?

    　(A) Two.

    　(B) Three.

    　(C) Four.

女：能請你給我一杯果汁嗎？

男：當然，還需要什麼嗎？

女：我想我要牛排還有一些炸薯片。

男：好。你想要點一份甜點嗎？

女：不了，這樣就好，謝謝你。

問題：這女生點了多少樣東西？

選項：(A) 兩樣。

　　　(B) 三樣。

　　　(C) 四樣。

答案 B

18. W: I've heard a lot about night markets in Taiwan. Is there one nearby?

    M: Yes. There's one only two blocks away from this hotel. It's just next to the train station.

    W: It's not far from here. Let's go! Can't wait to try the food and drinks!

    Q: Where are the speakers?

女：我已經聽說過很多關於臺灣的夜市。這附近有嗎？

男：有。這間飯店兩條街之外就有一個。它就在火車站旁邊。

女：離這裡不遠呢。走吧！等不及試試那裡的食物和飲料了！

問題：說話者在什麼地方？

(A) At the train station.

(B) In the night market.

(C) Near the hotel.

選項：(A) 在火車站。

(B) 在夜市裡。

(C) 在這間旅館附近。

答案 **C**

19. M: Excuse me. Could I use your bathroom?

W: Sure. Go down the hall, first door on the left.

M: Thanks.

Q: Where does the man want to go?

(A) The bedroom.

(B) The living room.

(C) The bathroom.

男：不好意思。我可以借用一下你的洗手間嗎？

女：當然。沿著走廊過去，左手邊第一個門。

男：謝謝。

問題：這男生要去哪裡？

選項：(A) 臥室。

(B) 起居室。

(C) 洗手間。

答案 **C**

20. M: Is it possible to talk to Sharon today?

W: I'm really sorry. She's going to be busy all day.

M: It'll just take 10 minutes. Can you help?

W: All right. Why don't you call back around 5 in the afternoon?

Q: When will Sharon be busy today?

(A) For the next 10 minutes.

(B) Around 5:00 p.m.

(C) All day.

男：今天我有可能跟莎朗談話嗎？

女：我真的很抱歉。她整天都將會很忙。

男：只需要差不多十分鐘而已。你能幫忙嗎？

女：好吧。你何不在下午五點左右再打來？

問題：莎朗在今天何時會很忙碌？

選項：(A) 接下來的十分鐘。

(B) 大約下午五點。

(C) 整天。

答案 **C**

21. M: Hi, Sara, I'm invited to Peter's party tomorrow night. Would you like to go with me?

W: Oh, I'd like to go, but tomorrow night I'm busy.

M: Can't you get out of it?

男：嗨，莎拉，我受邀請參加明天晚上彼得的派對。你要跟我一起去嗎？

女：噢，我很想去，不過明天晚上我很忙。

男：你不能把事情推掉嗎？

W: I promised my mother I'd have dinner with her tomorrow.

Q: Why did the woman refuse the man's invitation?

　　(A) She will attend another party.

　　(B) She will have dinner with her mother.

　　(C) She will be working late.

女：我答應我媽媽明天要和她一起吃晚餐。

問題：這女生為何拒絕這男生的邀請？

選項：(A) 她要參加另一個派對。

　　　(B) 她要和她母親一起吃晚餐。

　　　(C) 她要工作到很晚。

答案 B

22. W: Oh, I'm so full. The spaghetti was so tasty!

M: I like their tomato soup. You should try it next time.

W: Thank you for buying me dinner. I had a wonderful time.

M: It was my pleasure. So, would you like a ride home?

Q: What did the speakers do?

　　(A) The man took the woman home.

　　(B) They had dinner together.

　　(C) They went home by riding a bike.

女：哦，我好飽。那個義大利麵好美味！

男：我喜歡他們的番茄湯。你下次應該試試。

女：謝謝你請我吃晚餐。我過得很愉快。

男：這是我的榮幸。那麼，要不要送你一程回家呢？

問題：說話者做了什麼？

選項：(A) 這男生送這女生回家。

　　　(B) 他們一起吃晚餐。

　　　(C) 他們騎腳踏車回家。

答案 B

23. W: Jack, what's the matter?

M: Here, take a bite of my chicken sandwich.

W: Umm, I think the meat has gone bad.

M: That's what I think. I'm going to complain to the manager.

Q: What did Jack complain about?

　　(A) Drink.

　　(B) Service.

　　(C) Food.

女：傑克，你怎麼了？

男：嗯，你咬一口我的雞肉三明治。

女：唔，我想這肉已經壞掉了。

男：我想也是。我要去跟餐廳經理抱怨。

問題：傑克在抱怨什麼？

選項：(A) 飲料。

　　　(B) 服務。

　　　(C) 食物。

24. W: Who is that guy over there dressed in a blue shirt? I see him very often.

　　M: Oh, that's Martin. We work in the same office.

　　W: I've heard that he is kind to people. Is that true?

　　M: Yes. He always helps me out when I can't handle my work.

　　Q: Which is true about Martin?

　　　(A) He knows the woman.

　　　(B) He is unkind to others.

　　　(C) He works with the man.

女：那邊穿藍色襯衫的傢伙是誰？我很常看到他。

男：喔，那是馬丁。我們在同一個辦公室工作。

女：我聽說他對人很好。是真的嗎？

男：是啊。他總是在我無法應付工作時幫助我。

問題：哪個對馬丁的描述是正確的？

選項：(A) 他認識這女生。

　　　(B) 他對其他人很刻薄。

　　　(C) 他和這男生一起工作。

25. W: Carl, I think you look great in that pair of shoes.

　　M: Well, I'm afraid they are a little too small for me.

　　W: In that case, we need a larger size.

　　M: I think I should try the shoes in a size 6.

　　Q: What did the man say about the shoes?

　　　(A) They are not big enough.

　　　(B) The shoes in a size 5 fit his feet.

　　　(C) They don't suit him.

女：卡爾，我覺得那雙鞋很適合你。

男：嗯，可是它們對我而言太小雙了。

女：那麼，我們需要大一點的尺寸。

男：我覺得我應該試 6 號的鞋。

問題：關於這雙鞋這男生表示什麼？

選項：(A) 它們不夠大。

　　　(B) 5 號的鞋符合他的腳。

　　　(C) 它們不適合他。

第四部份：短文聽解

26. For question number 26, please look at the three pictures. Question number 26, Jessica is preparing for summer. What will Jessica do next?

第二十六題，請看這三張圖。第二十六題，潔西卡正在為夏天做準備。潔西卡接下來要做什麼？

Summer is coming. Jessica feels her hair is too long, so she will have her hair cut tonight. Before that, she will take a bath. She also plans to read ten books during summer vacation. Thus, she will go to the bookstore tomorrow.

(A) Read.

(B) Have her hair cut.

(C) Take a bath.

夏天即將來臨。潔西卡覺得她的頭髮太長了，所以她今晚將去剪頭髮。在那之前，她會先洗澡。她也計畫在暑假閱讀十本書。因此，她明天要去書局。

選項：(A) 看書。

(B) 剪頭髮。

(C) 洗澡。

答案　**C**

27. For question number 27, please look at the three pictures. Question number 27, listen to the following announcement. Where will you most probably hear this announcement?

Dear customers, there is a promotion in the produce section. All the fruits and vegetables are now on sale. It's a great chance. Don't miss it!

(A) In a hotel.

(B) At a gas station.

(C) In a supermarket.

第二十七題，請看這三張圖。第二十七題，注意聆聽接下來的廣播。你最有可能在哪裡聽到這則廣播？

親愛的顧客，蔬果區有促銷活動。所有的蔬菜和水果都在特賣。這是個好機會，千萬別錯過囉！

選項：(A) 旅館。

(B) 加油站。

(C) 超市。

答案　**C**

28. For question number 28, please look at the three pictures. Question number 28, listen to the following announcement. What is on sale now?

Your attention please. The bread is now on sale. It smells good and tastes delicious. It also goes well with milk. There is only a limited number of black bread available. First come, first served!

第二十八題，請看這三張圖。第二十八題，注意聆聽接下來的廣播。什麼東西正在特賣？

請注意，麵包現在正在特賣。它聞起來很香，吃起來很可口。它跟牛奶搭配起來也很美味。黑麥麵包的數量有限，先到先服務哦！

(A) Milk.

(B) Bread.

(C) Pizza.

選項：(A) 牛奶。

　　　(B) 麵包。

　　　(C) 披薩。

答案 **B**

29. For question number 29, please look at the three pictures. Question number 29, listen to the following message. What is Emily doing now?

Hi, Mom. This is Emily. I want to apologize for what I did this morning. I shouldn't have answered back and hurt your feelings. I will never do that again. Please, forgive me.

(A) Argue with her mother.

(B) Make a reservation.

(C) Make an apology.

第二十九題，請看這三張圖。第二十九題，注意聆聽接下來的留言。愛蜜莉現在正在做什麼？

嗨，媽，我是愛蜜莉。我想為我今天早上所做的事道歉。我不該回嘴的，也傷害了你。我再也不會那樣做了。請原諒我。

選項：(A) 跟母親吵架。

　　　(B) 訂位。

　　　(C) 道歉。

答案 **C**

30. For question number 30, please look at the three pictures. Question number 30, listen to the following short talk. What will most likely be the view from their hotel?

My friends and I are planning for a trip for this summer. We've found a hotel that is near a lake and decided to book a room. I think the view would be great! And we will visit a famous museum.

(A) An amusement park.

(B) A museum.

(C) A lake.

第三十題，請看這三張圖。第三十題，注意聆聽接下來的簡短談話。他們從旅館看到的景色最有可能是什麼樣子？

我和我的朋友們正在為今年的夏天計畫一趟旅行。我們已經找到一間在湖旁邊的旅館，並決定要訂房。我覺得那裡的風景一定很棒！而且我們將參觀一間著名的博物館。

選項：(A) 遊樂園。

　　　(B) 博物館。

　　　(C) 湖邊。

答案 **C**

Unit 4

第一部份：看圖辨義

1. For question number 1, please look at picture A. Question number 1:
   Where is this woman?
   (A) She is in the school.
   (B) She is in the factory.
   (C) She is in the supermarket.

   第一題，請看圖片 A。第一題：

   這女生在什麼地方？
   選項：(A) 她在學校裡。
   　　　(B) 她在工廠裡。
   　　　(C) 她在超級市場裡。

   答案　C

2. For question number 2, please look at picture B. Question number 2:
   What is the woman playing?
   (A) She is playing soccer.
   (B) She is playing tennis.
   (C) She is playing baseball.

   第二題，請看圖片 B。第二題：

   這女生正在進行什麼運動？
   選項：(A) 她正在踢足球。
   　　　(B) 她正在打網球。
   　　　(C) 她正在打棒球。

   答案　B

3. For questions number 3 and 4, please look at picture C. Question number 3:
   When will Jack see Dr. Wall?
   (A) 6:00 p.m.
   (B) 7:00 p.m.
   (C) 8:00 p.m.

   第三題及第四題，請看圖片 C。第三題：
   傑克什麼時候會跟瓦爾醫生見面？
   選項：(A) 晚上六點。
   　　　(B) 晚上七點。
   　　　(C) 晚上八點。

   答案　B

4. Question number 4, please look at picture C again.
   What information is given in the picture?
   (A) A weekly schedule.
   (B) Patients' name.
   (C) Lunch time.

   第四題，請再看一次圖片 C。

   圖片提供了什麼資訊？
   選項：(A) 一份週計畫表。
   　　　(B) 病人的名字。
   　　　(C) 午餐時間。

   答案　B

5. For question number 5, please look at picture D. Question number 5: Where are these people?

   (A) They are in the bank.

   (B) They are in the park.

   (C) They are in the classroom.

答案 C

第五題，請看圖片 D。第五題：

這些人在什麼地方？

選項：(A) 他們在銀行裡。

      (B) 他們在公園裡。

      (C) 他們在教室裡。

第二部份：問答

6. What's up?

   (A) It's up to you.

   (B) I'm up here.

   (C) Nothing much.

答案 C

最近有什麼新鮮事？

選項：(A) 看你的意思。

      (B) 我在上面這裡。

      (C) 沒什麼。

7. What do you do for a living?

   (A) I am a taxi driver.

   (B) I live in Taipei.

   (C) You can't do that.

答案 A

你做什麼工作呢？

選項：(A) 我是一位計程車司機。

      (B) 我住在臺北。

      (C) 你不能這麼做。

8. May I speak to Helen, please?

   (A) Please have her call me back later.

   (B) May I have your phone number?

   (C) Hang on. I'll get her.

答案 C

我可以跟海倫講話嗎？

選項：(A) 請她等一下回撥給我。

      (B) 能給我你的電話號碼嗎？

      (C) 別掛斷。我去叫她。

9. May I leave a message for Tom?

   (A) Sure. What should I tell him?

   (B) No, I will call him later.

   (C) Good morning, Tom.

答案 A

我可以留言給湯姆嗎？

選項：(A) 當然。你要我跟他說什麼？

      (B) 不，我等一下會打給他。

      (C) 早安，湯姆。

10. Could I use your cell phone?

   (A) Of course. I lost it.

   (B) Yes, it's mine.

我能借用一下你的手機嗎？

選項：(A) 當然。我的手機掉了。

      (B) 是的，那是我的。

(C) Sure. Here you are.

答案 **C**

11. Mr. Owens can see you at 11 o'clock tomorrow morning. Can you make it?
    (A) Great. I'll be there at 11.
    (B) Yes, tomorrow night will be fine.
    (C) No problem. What time?

答案 **A**

12. Come on! Have some more.
    (A) He is not coming.
    (B) OK. They're really delicious.
    (C) Why did you come?

答案 **B**

13. I like your new hair style.
    (A) You are not welcome.
    (B) That's nice of you to say so.
    (C) No, that's mine.

答案 **B**

14. I don't know how to put it, but . . . your music is really loud.
    (A) He is a great musician.
    (B) What are you looking for?
    (C) Gee, I'm really sorry.

答案 **C**

15. How did the test go?
    (A) I'm fine, thank you.
    (B) I think I did pretty well.
    (C) I will do my best.

答案 **B**

(C) 當然。拿去吧。

歐文斯先生在明天早上十一點可以見你。你能來嗎？
選項：(A) 很好。我將在十一點到。
　　　(B) 是的，明天晚上很好。
　　　(C) 沒問題。什麼時候？

來吧！再多吃一點。
選項：(A) 他沒來。
　　　(B) 好。它們真是美味。
　　　(C) 你為什麼來？

我喜歡你的新髮型。
選項：(A) 你不受歡迎。
　　　(B) 你這樣說真好。
　　　(C) 不，那是我的。

我不知道怎麼開口，不過…你的音樂實在太大聲。
選項：(A) 他是一個偉大的音樂家。
　　　(B) 你正在找什麼？
　　　(C) 天啊，我真的很抱歉。

考試如何？
選項：(A) 我很好，謝謝你。
　　　(B) 我想我考得還不錯。
　　　(C) 我會盡我所能。

16. M: Oh, Margret! I didn't know you were back from Taipei.

    W: Hi, Bob. I got home last night.

    M: I thought you would come back on Friday.

    W: I left earlier because of the typhoon.

    Q: When did Margret get home from Taipei?

    (A) Last Friday.

    (B) Last week.

    (C) Last night.

男：噢，瑪格麗特！我不知道你從臺北回來了。

女：嗨，鮑伯。我昨晚就回到家了。

男：我以為你星期五才會回來。

女：因為颱風，我提早離開了。

問題：瑪格麗特什麼時候從臺北回到家？

選項：(A) 上星期五。

(B) 上星期。

(C) 昨晚。

答案 **C**

17. W: I went to see my grandmother last Sunday.

    M: Did you have a lot of fun?

    W: Of course. I want to visit her more often. Can you believe that she's turning 80 next year? Time flies!

    M: True. We should spend some time with our family.

    Q: How old is the woman's grandmother?

    (A) 79 years old.

    (B) 80 years old.

    (C) 81 years old.

女：上星期天我去看我祖母。

男：你們有玩得很開心嗎？

女：當然，我想更常探望她。你能相信她明年就要八十歲了嗎？時光飛逝呀！

男：沒錯，我們應該花點時間陪伴我們的家人。

問題：這女生的祖母幾歲了？

選項：(A) 七十九歲。

(B) 八十歲。

(C) 八十一歲。

答案 **A**

18. W: May I help you? You look like you're lost.

    M: Yes, I am. I'm looking for the train station. Do you know where it is?

    W: Go straight and you will see a bakery. Then turn right and walk for

女：我可以幫你嗎？你看起來像是迷路了。

男：是的，我迷路了。我正在找火車站。你知道它在哪裡嗎？

女：直走，你會看到一間烘焙坊。接著右轉，再走兩個街區。

two blocks.

M: I see. Thank you so much.

Q: What does the woman want to do?

    (A) She wants to buy some food.

    (B) She wants to find the train station.

    (C) She wants to help the man.

男：我知道了。非常感謝你。

問題：這女生想要做什麼？

選項：(A) 她想要去買一些食物。

       (B) 她想要找火車站。

       (C) 她想要幫助這男生。

答案 **C**

19. M: Can I borrow the book you bought last week?

W: I haven't finished it yet. How about next week?

M: Sure. There's no hurry.

Q: What does the man want from the woman?

    (A) He wants to buy a book for the woman.

    (B) He wants to borrow a book from the woman.

    (C) He wants to lend the woman a book.

男：我可以跟你借那本你上星期買的書嗎？

女：我還沒看完。再等一個星期如何？

男：當然。我不急。

問題：這男生想從這女生那邊要什麼？

選項：(A) 他想買書給這女生。

       (B) 他想向這女生借書。

       (C) 他想把書借給這女生。

答案 **B**

20. W: Is it possible to see Dr. May this morning?

M: Sure. How about 11:30?

W: Could you make it a little earlier? My daughter has a fever.

M: I see. How about 10:00?

W: We'll be there. Thanks a lot.

Q: What time will the woman's daughter see the doctor?

    (A) 10:00 this morning.

女：今天早上我有可能請梅醫生看診嗎？

男：當然。十一點半如何？

女：可不可以早一點？我女兒發燒。

男：我了解。那十點如何？

女：我們會到。非常感謝。

問題：這女生的女兒什麼時候看醫生？

選項：(A) 今天早上十點。

(B) 10:30 this morning.

(C) 11:30 this morning.

(B) 今天早上十點半。

(C) 今天早上十一點半。

答案 A

21. W: How about another piece of chicken pie?

M: No, thanks. I'm really full.

W: Well, how about some ice cream for dessert?

M: All right, I think I can make some room for it.

Q: What will the man do next?

(A) Eat some ice cream.

(B) Eat a piece of pie.

(C) Eat nothing.

女：再來一片雞肉派如何？

男：不，謝了。我真的吃得很飽。

女：那麼，來一些冰淇淋作為甜點如何？

男：好吧，我想我還可以騰一點空間給它。

問題：這男生接下來要做什麼？

選項：(A) 吃一些冰淇淋。

(B) 吃一片派。

(C) 什麼都不吃。

答案 A

22. W: May I take your order, please?

M: Yes. I'd like a hamburger with fries.

W: Certainly. And anything to drink? How about a Coke?

M: No. Thanks. That's it.

Q: What does the man order?

(A) A hamburger only.

(B) A hamburger and fries.

(C) A hamburger, fries, and a Coke.

女：請問我能為你點餐了嗎？

男：可以。我要一個漢堡還有薯條。

女：當然可以。那要喝點什麼嗎？可樂如何？

男：不了，謝謝。這樣就好。

問題：這男生點了什麼餐點？

選項：(A) 只有一個漢堡。

(B) 一個漢堡和薯條。

(C) 一個漢堡、薯條和可樂。

答案 B

23. M: Hi, Jane. How did you like your trip to London?

W: Oh, everything was wonderful except for one thing.

M: What was that?

W: It rained most of the time. It made walking around more difficult.

男：嗨，珍。你到倫敦旅行的感覺如何？

女：喔，除了一件事以外，其他什麼都很好。

男：是什麼事？

女：一直在下雨。那使得參觀遊覽變得很麻煩。

Q: What did Jane complain about?　問題：珍抱怨什麼？

(A) Weather.　選項：(A) 天氣。

(B) Job.　(B) 工作。

(C) Traffic.　(C) 交通。

答案 A

24. M: Don't you just love her singing? I sure do.

男：你應該不會不喜歡她唱歌吧？我可是非常喜歡。

W: Me, too. She's got a wonderful voice.

女：我也很喜歡。她擁有非常棒的歌聲。

M: I think I'll buy her new album.

男：我想我會買她的新專輯。

Q: What are they talking about?　問題：他們正在談論什麼？

(A) A female singer.　選項：(A) 一個女歌手。

(B) A male singer.　(B) 一個男歌手。

(C) A photo album.　(C) 一本相簿。

答案 A

25. W: Tim, what do you think about this dress?

女：提姆，你覺得這件套裝如何？

M: You look great. Pink really looks great on you.

男：看起來很不錯。粉紅色真的很適合你。

W: Thanks. I like the style, too, but it's kind of expensive.

女：謝謝你。我也喜歡這種款式，不過它有點貴。

M: Don't worry about it. I can buy it for you as a gift.

男：別擔心了。我可以買給你當作禮物。

Q: What did the woman complain about the dress?

問題：這女生抱怨這件套裝的哪一點？

(A) The color.　選項：(A) 顏色。

(B) The style.　(B) 款式。

(C) The price.　(C) 價格。

答案 C

第四部份：短文聽解

26. For question number 26, please look at the three pictures. Question number 26, listen to the following message. What will Jimmy's mother most probably make?

Honey, don't forget today is Jimmy's 5th birthday. I bought some cookies and I will make him a cake. Maybe you can get him a robot or something. Be sure to come home for dinner. Bye.

(A) A robot.

(B) A cake.

(C) Cookies.

答案 **B**

第二十六題，請看這三張圖。第二十六題，注意聆聽接下來的留言。吉米的母親最有可能做什麼？

親愛的，別忘了今天是吉米五歲的生日。我買了一些餅乾，我也會做一個蛋糕給他。或許你可以買一個機器人或是別的東西給他。要回家吃晚餐哦。再見。

選項：(A) 機器人。

(B) 蛋糕。

(C) 餅乾。

27. For question number 27, please look at the three pictures. Question number 27, Andy can't find his white jacket. Where will Andy go after hearing the following announcement?

Attention please. A white jacket has been turned in to the lost-and-found. Once again, a white jacket has been turned in to the lost-and-found. Anyone missing a white jacket please go to the lost-and-found near the information center. Thank you.

(A) The lost-and-found.

(B) The emergency exit.

(C) The information center.

答案 **A**

第二十七題，請看這三張圖。第二十七題，安迪找不到他白色的夾克。聽到接下來的廣播後，安迪會去哪裡？

請注意。一件白色的夾克被送到失物招領處。再重覆一次，一件白色的夾克被送到失物招領處。遺失白色夾克的人請到靠近服務櫃檯的失物招領處認領，謝謝。

選項：(A) 失物招領。

(B) 緊急逃生口。

(C) 服務櫃檯。

28. For question number 28, please look at

第二十八題，請看這三張圖。第二十

the three pictures. Question number 28, listen to the following message for Justin. What will Betty most probably borrow from Justin?

Hi, Justin, this is Betty. I'm going to France next week, but my camera is broken! The technician told me that it takes at least five days to repair it. So, may I borrow your camera? I would appreciate it if you would lend me your camera.

(A) A jacket.

(B) A camera.

(C) Some money.

答案 B

29. For question number 29, please look at the three pictures. Question number 29, Penny just shared a picture on the Net. Where were Penny and her friends?

Penny posted a picture on her blog to keep a record of her wonderful memory with her friends. Penny and her friends stood in the middle of the picture, and the background is a merry-go-round.

(A) A supermarket.

(B) A department store.

(C) An amusement park.

答案 C

30. For question number 30, please look at the three pictures. Question number 30, listen to the following message. Where will Monica most probably go tonight?

八題，注意聆聽接下來給賈斯汀的留言。貝蒂最有可能跟賈斯汀借什麼？

嗨，賈斯汀，我是貝蒂。我下禮拜要去法國，但是我的相機壞了！維修人員告訴我說要修好它至少要花上五天。所以，我可以跟你借相機嗎？如果你願意借我相機的話，我會很感激的。

選項：(A) 一件外套。
　　　(B) 一臺相機。
　　　(C) 一些錢。

第二十九題，請看這三張圖。第二十九題，佩妮剛剛在網路上分享了一張照片。佩妮和她的朋友們當時在哪裡？

佩妮貼了一張照片在她的部落格上，來記錄她和她的朋友們的美好回憶。佩妮和她的朋友們站在照片的中間，背景是一個旋轉木馬。

選項：(A) 超市。
　　　(B) 百貨公司。
　　　(C) 遊樂園。

第三十題，請看這三張圖。第三十題，注意聆聽接下來的留言。莫妮卡今晚最有可能去哪裡？

Hi, Mom. It's me, Monica. I'm going to the library with Mark now. And I will be late tonight since one of my classmates invited me to join her birthday party. Don't worry about me. After the party, I will go straight home.

(A) A movie theater.

(B) A wedding.

(C) A birthday party.

答案 C

嗨，媽，我是莫妮卡。我現在要跟馬克去圖書館。我今天會晚一點回去因為我同學邀請我去參加她的生日派對。別擔心，派對過後我就會直接回家。

選項：(A) 電影院。

(B) 婚禮。

(C) 生日派對。

第一部份：看圖辨義

1. For question number 1, please look at picture A. Question number 1:
   What is on the man's right?
   (A) Music Tower.
   (B) Mary's Flowers.
   (C) QBC Department Store.

   第一題，請看圖片 A。第一題：

   這男生的右邊有什麼？
   選項：(A) 音樂城。
   　　　(B) 瑪莉花店。
   　　　(C) QBC 百貨公司。

   答案　**C**

2. For questions number 2 and 3, please look at picture B. Question number 2:
   Where will this schedule most likely be seen?
   (A) In a railroad station.
   (B) In a gas station.
   (C) In a post office.

   第二題及第三題，請看圖片 B。第二題：

   會在哪裡看到這個車次表？
   選項：(A) 一個火車站裡。
   　　　(B) 一間加油站裡。
   　　　(C) 一間郵局裡。

   答案　**A**

3. Question number 3, please look at picture B again. When is the train to Kaohsiung?
   (A) 8:20.
   (B) 9:45.
   (C) 10:00.

   第三題，請再看一次圖片 B。到高雄的列車是幾點？
   選項：(A) 八點二十分。
   　　　(B) 九點四十五分。
   　　　(C) 十點。

   答案　**C**

4. For questions number 4 and 5, please look at picture C. Question number 4:
   What's happening in the picture?
   (A) James is taking an order.
   (B) Paul is having a meal.
   (C) They are watching the flowers.

   第四題及第五題，請看圖片 C。第四題：

   圖片中發生什麼事？
   選項：(A) 詹姆士正在點餐。
   　　　(B) 保羅正在用餐。
   　　　(C) 他們在觀賞花。

   答案　**A**

5. Question number 5, please look at picture C again. What is Paul most likely saying to James?

    (A) I think the trousers look nice.

    (B) Sure. Please wait for a couple of minutes.

    (C) I would like to have a chicken sandwich.

第五題，請再看一次圖片 C。保羅最有可能對詹姆士說什麼？

選項：(A) 我想這褲子看起來不錯。

      (B) 當然。請稍候幾分鐘。

      (C) 我想要一個雞肉三明治。

答案 **C**

第二部份：問答

6. How have you been?

    (A) I have been to Tainan.

    (B) Nice to meet you.

    (C) Not bad at all. And you?

最近如何？

選項：(A) 我去過臺南。

      (B) 很高興認識你。

      (C) 還不錯。你呢？

答案 **C**

7. When should I hand in my homework?

    (A) The sooner the better.

    (B) I'm sorry to hear that.

    (C) You should do your homework after school.

我什麼時候該繳交作業？

選項：(A) 越快越好。

      (B) 聽到這個我很遺憾。

      (C) 你要在放學後做功課。

答案 **A**

8. Sorry, I don't know how to get there, either.

    (A) I've never heard of that place.

    (B) That's OK. I'll ask someone else.

    (C) Sure. You won't miss it.

抱歉，我也不知道怎麼到那邊。

選項：(A) 我從來沒聽過那個地方。

      (B) 沒關係。我去問別人。

      (C) 當然。你不會錯過的。

答案 **B**

9. Wanna have some ice cream? It tastes really good.

    (A) Sure. You can eat what you want.

    (B) Well, but I'm on a diet.

    (C) Can I have a bite of your cake?

想來點冰淇淋嗎？它嘗起來很棒。

選項：(A) 當然。你可以吃你想吃的。

      (B) 嗯…不過我在節食。

      (C) 我能吃一口你的蛋糕嗎？

10. Could you turn on the radio for me?

    (A) Yes, I wanted the radio.

    (B) Sure, no problem.

    (C) No, thanks.

你可以幫我把收音機打開嗎？

選項：(A) 是的，我要這臺收音機。

(B) 當然，沒問題。

(C) 不，謝了。

11. I'm afraid you can't use my motorcycle.

    (A) Why not?

    (B) Riding a motorcycle is fun.

    (C) Me, too.

恐怕你不能使用我的機車了。

選項：(A) 為何不行？

(B) 騎機車很好玩。

(C) 我也是。

12. What beautiful eyes you have!

    (A) I'm glad you are.

    (B) Do you really like it?

    (C) Oh, thank you so much.

你的眼睛真漂亮！

選項：(A) 很高興你是這樣。

(B) 你真的喜歡嗎？

(C) 噢，非常謝謝你。

13. I really don't know how to thank you.

    (A) It was nothing.

    (B) Thank you very much.

    (C) You can say that again!

我不知道該怎麼謝謝你。

選項：(A) 那沒什麼。

(B) 非常謝謝你。

(C) 你說得一點也沒錯！

14. How do you like the book you bought yesterday?

    (A) I prefer watching TV to reading a book.

    (B) I was sick yesterday.

    (C) I like it very much.

你喜歡昨天買的書嗎？

選項：(A) 跟讀書相比，我比較喜歡看電視。

(B) 我昨天生病了。

(C) 我非常喜歡它。

15. Would you like to go to a movie with me after school?

放學之後你願意跟我去看電影嗎？

(A) I'd like to, but I have football practice today.
(B) It was a good movie.
(C) Sure. Go straight and turn right, and you'll see it.

選項：(A) 我很想，不過我今天有美式足球的練習。
(B) 那是一部好電影。
(C) 當然。直走後右轉，你就會看到了。

答案 **A**

第三部份：簡短對話

16. M: Where do you live?
    W: No. 1738, West Street.
    M: What? No wonder I run into you so often. I just live across the street.
    W: Next time you can come to my place and have fun together!
    Q: What are these people mainly discussing?
    (A) Vendors on West Street.
    (B) Where they live.
    (C) When they first met.

男：你住在哪裡？
女：西街 1738 號。
男：什麼？難怪我常遇見你，我就住在街道對面而已。
女：下次你可以來我家，我們可以一起玩！
問題：說話者主要在討論什麼？

選項：(A) 西街的攤販。
(B) 他們住的地方。
(C) 他們第一次見面的時候。

答案 **B**

17. M: Excuse me. Could you tell me how to get to the train station? I'm in a hurry.
    W: Yes. The best way is to take a bus. It will take a long time to walk from here.
    M: Oh, then which bus should I take?
    W: You can take No. 364 or 287.
    Q: Why does the woman suggest taking a bus?
    (A) Taking a bus is more convenient.
    (B) The man doesn't like to walk.
    (C) The man doesn't have much time.

男：不好意思。你能告訴我如何到火車站嗎？我在趕時間。
女：是的。最好的方式就是搭公車。從這裡走過去會花很多時間。
男：哦，那我該搭乘哪輛公車？
女：你可以搭乘 364 或 287。
問題：為什麼這女生建議搭乘公車？

選項：(A) 搭乘公車比較方便。
(B) 這男生不喜歡走路。
(C) 這男生沒有很多時間。

18. M: Is Michael there?

   W: Sorry. We don't have a Michael here.

   M: Is this 784-7586?

   W: No, it's 784-7568. I think you have the wrong number.

   Q: What is the woman's phone number?
     (A) 784-7586.
     (B) 784-7568.
     (C) 786-7586.

男：麥可在嗎？

女：抱歉。這裡沒有麥可這個人。

男：你那邊是 784-7586 嗎？

女：不，是 784-7568。我想你撥錯號碼了。

問題：這女生的電話號碼是什麼？
選項：(A) 784-7586。
　　　(B) 784-7568。
　　　(C) 786-7586。

19. M: May I help you?

   W: Yes. I would like to try on that red T-shirt over there. Could you take it for me?

   M: Sure. Here you go.

   W: Thanks.

   Q: Where does the conversation take place?
     (A) In a hotel.
     (B) In a department store.
     (C) In a coffee shop.

男：需要幫忙嗎？

女：是，我想試穿那邊的那件紅色 T 恤。你能幫我拿嗎？

男：當然，給你。

女：謝謝。

問題：這個對話發生在哪裡？

選項：(A) 在旅館裡。
　　　(B) 在百貨公司裡。
　　　(C) 在咖啡廳裡。

20. M: Mr. Shaw's office. May I help you?

   W: Yes. I'd like to have a talk with Mr. Shaw.

   M: Well, Mr. Shaw is in Hong Kong and he won't be back until the end of this month.

   W: Oh, that's too bad. Thanks anyway.

   Q: When will Mr. Shaw be back?

男：蕭先生辦公室。我能為您效勞嗎？

女：是的。我想跟蕭先生談話。

男：嗯，蕭先生人在香港，要到本月底才會回來。

女：噢，太糟了。不過還是謝謝你。

問題：蕭先生什麼時候回來？

(A) Tomorrow.

(B) Later this month.

(C) Next month.

選項：(A) 明天。

(B) 本月底。

(C) 下個月。

答案　**B**

21. M: Would you like some coffee?

W: Sure, thanks.

M: Would you like to have sugar and cream in it?

W: No, just black will be fine.

Q: How did the woman want her coffee?

(A) She'd like to have sugar and cream in it.

(B) She didn't want sugar or cream in it.

(C) She'd like to have black tea.

男：要來一些咖啡嗎？

女：好啊，謝謝你。

男：要加糖和奶精嗎？

女：不，黑咖啡就好。

問題：這女生要怎麼樣的咖啡？

選項：(A) 她想要加糖和奶精。

(B) 她不要加糖或奶精。

(C) 她想要喝紅茶。

答案　**B**

22. W: Hi, Golden Gate Restaurant. May I help you?

M: Yes. My name is Stanley Lewis, and I'd like to reserve a table for 10.

W: Sure. For what day?

M: Next Thursday night.

Q: Why does Mr. Lewis make the phone call?

(A) He wants to work there.

(B) He will get there at 10.

(C) He wants to book a table.

女：嗨，這裡是金門餐廳。有什麼我可以效勞的嗎？

男：是的。我的名字是史坦利‧路易斯，我想訂十個人的位子。

女：好的。哪一天？

男：下星期四的晚上。

問題：路易斯先生為什麼打電話？

選項：(A) 他想在那裡工作。

(B) 他十點會到那裡。

(C) 他想要訂位子。

答案　**C**

23. M: I'm afraid I'll be late by 15 minutes.

W: That's OK. I know it's rush hour.

M: I should have taken a taxi instead of a bus.

男：我恐怕會晚到十五分鐘。

女：沒關係。我知道現在是尖峰時間。

男：我應該搭計程車，不應該搭公車。

Q: What did the man complain about?　問題：這男生在抱怨什麼？
　(A) Traffic.　選項：(A) 交通。
　(B) Education.　　　(B) 教育。
　(C) Environment.　　　(C) 環境。

答案　**A**

24. W: This is our latest model.　女：這是我們最新的樣式。
M: Wow, NT$5,000! I'm not ready to pay that much.　男：哇，新臺幣五千元！我可沒打算花那麼多錢。
W: Well, let me show you our other models.　女：那麼，讓我秀給你看一些其他的樣式。
Q: How did the man feel about the latest model?　問題：這男生覺得最新樣式如何？
　(A) Too big.　選項：(A) 太大了。
　(B) Too small.　　　(B) 太小了。
　(C) Too expensive.　　　(C) 太貴了。

答案　**C**

25. M: What kind of stories do you like the best?　男：你最喜歡哪一種故事？
W: I like ghost stories the best. How about you?　女：我最喜歡鬼故事。你呢？
M: I like stories that are romantic, especially stories about couples.　男：我喜歡浪漫的故事，尤其是關於情侶的故事。
W: Are you serious? Those are my least favorite stories.　女：你是認真的嗎？那些是我最不喜歡的故事。
Q: What kind of stories does the man like the best?　問題：這男生最喜歡哪一種故事？
　(A) Love stories.　選項：(A) 愛情故事。
　(B) Ghost stories.　　　(B) 鬼故事。
　(C) History stories.　　　(C) 歷史故事。

答案　**A**

26. For question number 26, please look at the three pictures. Question number 26, listen to the following message for Peggy. When is Peggy's birthday?

    Dear Peggy, today is April Fools' Day, which is your birthday! I do hope that everything goes well with you. The box on the dinner table is your birthday present and I hope you will like it. Happy birthday!

    (A) April 1st.
    (B) April 7th.
    (C) December 25th.

第二十六題，請看這三張圖。第二十六題，請注意聆聽接下來給佩姬的留言。佩姬的生日在什麼時候？

親愛的佩姬，今天是愚人節，也就是你的生日！我希望你事事都順心。在餐桌上的盒子是你的生日禮物，希望你會喜歡。生日快樂！

選項：(A) 四月一日。
　　　(B) 四月七日。
　　　(C) 十二月二十五日。

答案　**A**

27. For question number 27, please look at the three pictures. Question number 27, listen to the following short talk. What will Fiona most probably do?

    Fiona worked to a very tight schedule, and she has worked more than 14 hours. She was too tired to go to the department store with her sister. She just wanted to take a rest.

    (A) Go to sleep.
    (B) Go shopping.
    (C) Go swimming.

第二十七題，請看這三張圖。第二十七題，注意聆聽接下來的簡短對談。費歐娜最有可能做什麼？

費歐娜的工作很緊湊，而且她已經持續工作超過十四個小時了。她太累了以至於無法跟她姊姊去逛百貨公司。她只想要休息。

選項：(A) 睡覺。
　　　(B) 逛街。
　　　(C) 游泳。

答案　**A**

28. For question number 28, please look at the three pictures. Question number 28, Debby is telling her friend about what happened last night. Where did Debby

第二十八題，請看這三張圖。第二十八題，黛比正在告訴她的朋友昨晚發生什麼事。黛比在回家前去了哪裡？

go before going home?

I found a purse on my way home. I didn't know whose it was. There are several thousand dollars and some credit cards in it. So, I handed it over to the police.

(A) The police station.

(B) The music hall.

(C) The school.

答案 **A**

29. For question number 29, please look at the three pictures. Question number 29, listen to the following announcement. When is the closing time of the bookstore?

Attention all customers! Now it's 9:50. We'll be closing in 10 minutes. Thank you for shopping with us and we hope we will have the chance to serve you again. Thank you.

(A) 9:50.

(B) 10:00.

(C) 10:10.

答案 **B**

30. For question number 30, please look at the three pictures. Question number 30, listen to the following announcement. What's the top prize?

Attention all customers! We're having a prize drawing today. You will get a slip of paper and please write down your name, phone number and address on it and drop it into this box. The top prize

---

我在回家的路上發現一個皮包。我不知道這是誰的。裡面有好幾千塊跟數張信用卡。所以我把皮包交給警察。

選項：(A) 警局。

　　　(B) 音樂廳。

　　　(C) 學校。

第二十九題，請看這三張圖。第二十九題，注意聆聽接下來的廣播。這家書局的打烊時間是什麼時候？

所有的顧客請注意！現在時間是九點五十分。我們將於十分鐘後結束營業。謝謝您的光臨，希望我們能有再次服務您的機會。謝謝您。

選項：(A) 九點五十分。

　　　(B) 十點。

　　　(C) 十點十分。

第三十題，請看這三張圖。第三十題，注意聆聽接下來的廣播。頭獎是什麼？

所有的顧客請注意！我們今天有抽獎活動。您將拿到一張紙條，請寫下您的姓名，電話和地址並且丟入這個箱子裡。頭獎是一輛全新的汽車。

is a brand new car.

(A) A notebook.

(B) A bike.

(C) A car.

答案　**C**

選項：(A) 筆記型電腦。

　　　(B) 腳踏車。

　　　(C) 汽車。

第一部份：看圖辨義

1. For question number 1, please look at picture A. Question number 1:

   Who are these two women?

   (A) They are meeting for the first time.

   (B) They are shaking hands.

   (C) They are old friends.

第一題，請看圖片 A。第一題：

這兩個女生是什麼人？

選項：(A) 她們第一次見面。

　　　(B) 她們正在握手。

　　　(C) 她們是老朋友。

> 答案　**C**

2. For questions number 2 and 3, please look at picture B. Question number 2:

   What information is given on the screen?

   (A) The names of each team.

   (B) Phone numbers.

   (C) The price of tickets.

第二題及第三題，請看圖片 B。第二題：

這個螢幕上提供了什麼資訊？

選項：(A) 各隊的名稱。

　　　(B) 電話號碼。

　　　(C) 門票的價格。

> 答案　**A**

3. Question number 3, please look at picture B again. Which team wins the game?

   (A) Taipei Bears.

   (B) Shanghai Tigers.

   (C) They get the same score.

第三題，請再看一次圖片 B。哪一隊贏得比賽？

選項：(A) 臺北熊隊。

　　　(B) 上海虎隊。

　　　(C) 他們得到同分。

> 答案　**A**

4. For question number 4, please look at picture C. Question number 4:

   What is the woman doing?

   (A) She is eating fried chicken.

   (B) She is washing dishes.

   (C) She is drinking juice.

第四題，請看圖片 C。第四題：

這女生在做什麼？

選項：(A) 她正在吃雞塊。

　　　(B) 她正在洗盤子。

　　　(C) 她正在喝果汁。

> 答案　**C**

5. For question number 5, please look at picture D. Question number 5:

第五題，請看圖片 D。第五題：

How is the weather in this picture? | 圖裡的天氣如何？
(A) It's very cold. | 選項：(A) 非常冷。
(B) It's very hot. | (B) 非常熱。
(C) It rains a lot. | (C) 雨下得很大。

答案 **A**

第二部份：問答

6. How is everything? | 最近過得如何？
   (A) Fine, thanks. How about you? | 選項：(A) 很好，謝謝你。你呢？
   (B) The weather is beautiful. | (B) 天氣很不錯。
   (C) You are welcome. | (C) 不客氣。

答案 **A**

7. Where do you work? | 你在哪裡工作？
   (A) I enjoy my work very much. | 選項：(A) 我很喜歡我的工作。
   (B) I work in a bookstore. | (B) 我在書局工作。
   (C) I work five days a week. | (C) 我每星期工作五天。

答案 **B**

8. Where is the ticket office? | 售票處在哪裡？
   (A) The next movie will begin at 2:30. | 選項：(A) 下場電影於兩點半開演。
   (B) It's NT$250 for one person. | (B) 每人新臺幣兩百五十元。
   (C) Go down the stairs to B1. | (C) 下樓梯到地下一樓。

答案 **C**

9. Mr. Wang, please. | 麻煩請王先生聽電話。
   (A) She's not in now. | 選項：(A) 她現在不在。
   (B) Speaking. | (B) 請說。
   (C) No, thanks. | (C) 不，謝了。

答案 **B**

10. Do you mind coming back at 2 o'clock this afternoon? | 你介意今天下午兩點再過來一趟嗎？
    (A) No, not at all. | 選項：(A) 不，一點也不介意。
    (B) Yes, please. | (B) 是的，請。
    (C) No, it was yesterday afternoon. | (C) 不，那是昨天下午。

11. Would you like to come over tonight for dinner?

    (A) Sounds great.

    (B) Dinner was good.

    (C) He will come over tomorrow.

你願意今天晚上過來吃晚餐嗎？

選項：(A) 聽起來很不錯。

　　　(B) 晚餐很好。

　　　(C) 他明天將會過來。

12. Would you like to have some coffee?

    (A) Yes, I want orange juice.

    (B) No, I'd like it black.

    (C) That'd be nice. Thank you.

你想要喝一些咖啡嗎？

選項：(A) 是的，我要柳橙汁。

　　　(B) 不，我喜歡黑咖啡。

　　　(C) 好啊。謝謝你。

13. Do you like sweets?

    (A) Yes, I do. Chocolate is my favorite.

    (B) The cake is too sweet.

    (C) Pass the sugar, please.

你喜歡甜食嗎？

選項：(A) 喜歡。巧克力是我的最愛。

　　　(B) 這蛋糕太甜了。

　　　(C) 請把糖遞過來。

14. Oh, I forgot to bring you a book.

    (A) Never mind.

    (B) Be my guest.

    (C) It's hard to say.

哦，我忘了帶一本書給你。

選項：(A) 沒關係。

　　　(B) 請便。

　　　(C) 這很難說。

15. Susan, please come to my office after school.

    (A) Sure, Ms. Lin.

    (B) No, never mind.

    (C) Yes, you're right.

蘇珊，請在放學之後來我的辦公室。

選項：(A) 是的，林老師。

　　　(B) 不，別擔心。

　　　(C) 是的，你是對的。

第三部份：簡短對話

16. M: What do you want for your dessert?

    W: I like cakes.

男：你想吃什麼甜點？

女：我喜歡蛋糕。

M: But they don't serve cakes. How about some ice cream?

W: No, thanks. That's OK.

Q: What will the woman have for her dessert?

   (A) Cakes.

   (B) Ice cream.

   (C) Nothing.

男：但是他們沒有供應蛋糕。冰淇淋如何？

女：不了，謝謝。沒關係。

問題：這女生會吃什麼甜點？

選項：(A) 蛋糕。

   (B) 冰淇淋。

   (C) 什麼都不吃。

答案 **C**

17. M: Where are you going?

W: I will go to the convenience store and buy some food.

M: I wonder if you could mail a letter for me.

W: Sure thing.

Q: What did the man ask the woman to do?

   (A) To buy him a drink.

   (B) To send a mail for him.

   (C) To get some food for him.

男：你要去哪裡？

女：我要去便利商店買一些食物。

男：我在想你是否能幫我寄一封信。

女：沒問題。

問題：這男生要求這女生做什麼？

選項：(A) 幫他買一杯飲料。

   (B) 幫他寄一封信。

   (C) 幫他買一些食物。

答案 **B**

18. M: Hello, is Louis there?

W: Sorry, he is out.

M: Can I leave a message for him?

W: Sure. Go ahead.

Q: What will the woman do?

   (A) The woman will tell the man where Louis is.

   (B) The woman will call Louis right away.

   (C) The woman will take a message for Louis.

男：喂，請問路易在嗎？

女：抱歉，他不在。

男：我可以留個信息給他嗎？

女：當然。請說。

問題：這女生將要做什麼？

選項：(A) 這女生將會告訴這男生路易在哪裡。

   (B) 這女生將會立刻打電話給路易。

   (C) 這女生將會幫路易留信息。

19. W: Jason, can you do me a favor?

M: Sure, what is it?

W: Could you give me a ride to the airport tomorrow?

M: No problem. What time should I pick you up?

Q: What will Jason do for the woman tomorrow?

(A) Drive the woman to the airport.

(B) Take the woman out for a ride.

(C) Pick up the woman at the airport.

女：傑森，你可以幫我一個忙嗎？

男：當然。是什麼事？

女：你明天能載我到機場嗎？

男：沒問題。我應該什麼時候去接你？

問題：傑森明天將要為這女生做什麼？

選項：(A) 載這女生到機場。

(B) 帶這女生出去兜風。

(C) 到機場接這女生。

20. M: Take it easy. It's only a test.

W: But if I fail, I will have to spend all summer studying it again.

M: Well, just do your best and you will pass.

W: OK. But I think I'll have to burn the midnight oil tonight.

Q: What is the woman worrying about?

(A) A match.

(B) A speech.

(C) A test.

男：放輕鬆。那只不過是一次考試。

女：但如果我沒有通過，我將必須花整個夏天重新研讀。

男：嗯，只要你盡全力，一定會及格的。

女：好。不過我想我今晚必須要熬夜讀書了。

問題：這女生擔心什麼？

選項：(A) 一場比賽。

(B) 一場演講。

(C) 一次考試。

21. W: Why are you so late today?

M: Sorry. I was caught in a traffic jam.

W: Never mind. But don't be late again.

M: OK.

Q: What happened to the man?

(A) He slept late.

(B) He was caught in heavy traffic.

女：你為什麼今天這麼晚？

男：抱歉，我遇上交通堵塞。

女：沒關係。但下次別再遲到。

男：好。

問題：這男生發生什麼事？

選項：(A) 他睡太晚。

(B) 他塞在車陣中。

(C) He forgot to set the alarm.

(C) 他忘記設定鬧鐘。

> 答案 **B**

22. M: This set of shelves is the most popular one. Do you like it?

W: Yes, but I don't think the size is perfect for my room. It's too big.

M: How about this one?

W: Oh, great. It's small enough to fit in my room. I'll take it.

Q: Where are the speakers?

(A) In a bakery.

(B) In a furniture store.

(C) In a stationery store.

男：這組架子是最受歡迎的。你喜歡嗎？

女：喜歡，但我不認為這尺寸對我的房間而言是完美的。它太大了。

男：那這組怎麼樣？

女：噢，很好。它夠小，可以適用在我的房間裡。我買了。

問題：說話者在什麼地方？

選項：(A) 在烘焙坊。

(B) 在家具店。

(C) 在文具店。

> 答案 **B**

23. M: Laura, how have you been recently?

W: Not too good. Actually, I feel tired all the time.

M: Did you see a doctor?

W: No. Maybe I should have a checkup at the hospital.

Q: What are these people mainly discussing?

(A) Work.

(B) Health.

(C) Hospital.

男：蘿拉，你最近如何？

女：不太好。事實上，我一直覺得很疲倦。

男：你看過醫生了嗎？

女：沒有。也許我應該到醫院去檢查一下。

問題：說話者主要在討論什麼？

選項：(A) 工作。

(B) 健康。

(C) 醫院。

> 答案 **B**

24. W: Hi, may I help you?

M: Yes. I bought these shoes here yesterday. They're too large for me. I'd like to change them for a smaller size.

W: Sure. Wait a moment, please.

女：嗨，有什麼我可以效勞嗎？

男：喔。我昨天在這裡買了這些鞋。它們對我而言太大了。我想要換小一點的尺寸。

女：好。請等一下。

Q: Why is the man NOT satisfied with the shoes?

(A) Wrong color.

(B) Wrong style.

(C) Wrong size.

問題：這男生為什麼不滿意這些鞋子？

選項：(A) 顏色不對。

(B) 款式不對。

(C) 尺寸不對。

答案 **C**

25. M: Honey, I don't think this dress looks good on you.

W: Why? Is it because of the shoes I wear today?

M: Well, because your skin is a little dark, pink is really not your color.

W: All right. I'll try on another one.

Q: How does the man like the dress?

(A) He thinks the dress doesn't match the woman's shoes.

(B) He thinks the color of the dress isn't right for the woman.

(C) He thinks the dress is too expensive.

男：親愛的，我覺得這件套裝穿在你身上並不好看。

女：為什麼？是因為我今天穿的鞋子嗎？

男：嗯，因為你的膚色有點深，粉紅色真的不適合你。

女：好吧，我去試穿另外一件。

問題：這男生對這件套裝感覺如何？

選項：(A) 他覺得這件套裝跟這女生的鞋子不搭配。

(B) 他覺得這件套裝的顏色跟這女生不合。

(C) 他覺得這件套裝太貴。

答案 **B**

第四部份：短文聽解

26. For question number 26, please look at the three pictures. Question number 26, listen to the following announcement. Where will you most probably hear this announcement?

Attention, please. All tickets for the show have been sold out. Tickets will not be available until tomorrow morning. For further information, please

第二十六題，請看這三張圖。第二十六題，注意聆聽接下來的廣播。你最有可能在哪裡聽到這則廣播？

請注意！這場表演所有的門票都已經售完了。要到明天早上才會有可售的門票。欲知詳情，請見我們的官方網站。若造成任何不便，我們深表歉意。

visit our official website. We apologize for any inconvenience caused.

(A) Information center.

(B) A restaurant.

(C) The ticket office.

答案 C

選項：(A) 服務櫃檯。

(B) 餐廳。

(C) 售票處。

27. For question number 27, please look at the three pictures. Question number 27, listen to the following short talk. Where will Karen most probably go?

Karen can't go to school because she is sick. She has a fever and her nose is running. She feels very uncomfortable, so she decides to go to a doctor.

(A) The hospital.

(B) The post office.

(C) The forest.

答案 A

第二十七題，請看這三張圖。第二十七題，注意聆聽接下來的簡短談話。凱倫最有可能去哪裡？

凱倫不能去上學因為她生病了。她發燒和流鼻水。她覺得非常的不舒服，所以她決定去看醫生。

選項：(A) 醫院。

(B) 郵局。

(C) 森林。

28. For question number 28, please look at the three pictures. Question number 28, listen to the following message for Jessica. What will Jessica most probably have for dinner?

Jessica, I know you've been working so hard recently, so I've reserved a table for two at your favorite Japanese restaurant tonight. We'll have a lot of fun! I'll pick you up at 6 o'clock. See you then.

(A) Hamburger.

(B) Sushi.

(C) Spaghetti.

第二十八題，請看這三張圖。第二十八題，注意聆聽接下來給潔西卡的留言。潔西卡的晚餐最有可能吃什麼？

潔西卡，我知道你最近很努力地工作，所以我今晚在你最喜歡的日式餐廳訂了兩個位子。我們會玩得很愉快！我六點的時候會去接你，到時見囉。

選項：(A) 漢堡。

(B) 壽司。

(C) 義大利麵。

29. For question number 29, please look at the three pictures. Question number 29, listen to the following announcement. Where will you most probably hear this announcement?

Good morning passengers. San Min Airlines Flight CI915 to Hong Kong is now boarding. All passengers for Flight CI915 please proceed to Gate 10.

(A) At the airport.

(B) In the school.

(C) In the bank.

第二十九題，請看這三張圖。第二十九題，注意聆聽接下來的廣播。你最有可能在哪裡聽到這則廣播？

各位乘客早安。三民航空飛往香港的班機 CI915 現在要登機了。搭乘 CI915 班機的旅客請前往 10 號門。

選項：(A) 機場裡。
　　　(B) 學校裡。
　　　(C) 銀行裡。

30. For question number 30, please look at the three pictures. Question number 30, a man is leaving a phone message for his father. Where will the man most likely go next?

Hi, Dad. I just finished the basketball training. I am going to study right now because the final exams are coming. By the way, are you coming home late tonight? Send me a message. The place is really quiet, so I can't pick up the phone there.

(A) The gym.

(B) The library.

(C) The art museum.

第三十題，請看這三張圖。第三十題，一位男生正在留語音訊息給他的父親。這男生接下來最有可能去哪裡？

嗨，爸。我剛結束籃球訓練。我現在要去讀書，因為期末考試即將來臨。順便問一下，你今晚會比較晚回家嗎？傳訊息給我。那個地方非常安靜，所以我沒辦法在那裡接電話。

選項：(A) 體育館。
　　　(B) 圖書館。
　　　(C) 美術館。

第一部份：看圖辨義

1. For question number 1, please look at picture A. Question number 1:
   Where are they?
   (A) They are in a classroom.
   (B) They are in a coffee shop.
   (C) They are in a bookstore.

   第一題，請看圖片 A。第一題：
   他們在什麼地方？
   選項：(A) 他們在教室裡。
   　　　(B) 他們在咖啡廳裡。
   　　　(C) 他們在書店裡。

   答案　**B**

2. For questions number 2 and 3, please look at picture B. Question number 2:
   What are they talking about?
   (A) A building.
   (B) A park.
   (C) An airport.

   第二題及第三題，請看圖片 B。第二題：
   他們正在談論什麼？
   選項：(A) 一棟建築物。
   　　　(B) 一個公園。
   　　　(C) 一個機場。

   答案　**A**

3. Question number 3, please look at picture B again. What is the woman most likely saying to the man?
   (A) Have you ever been there?
   (B) The mountain is very high.
   (C) Can you take a photo of us?

   第三題，請再看一次圖片 B。這女生最有可能對這男生說什麼？
   選項：(A) 你去過那裡嗎？
   　　　(B) 這座山非常高。
   　　　(C) 你能幫我們拍張照嗎？

   答案　**A**

4. For question number 4, please look at picture C. Question number 4:
   What is the girl eating for her lunch?
   (A) Sandwiches.
   (B) Steak.
   (C) Noodles.

   第四題，請看圖片 C。第四題：
   這女孩午餐吃什麼？
   選項：(A) 三明治。
   　　　(B) 牛排。
   　　　(C) 麵。

   答案　**A**

5. For question number 5, please look at

   第五題，請看圖片 D。第五題：

picture D. Question number 5:

What are they doing?

(A) They are playing football.

(B) They are studying English.

(C) They are having lunch.

> 他們正在做什麼？
>
> 選項：(A) 他們正在打美式足球。
>
> (B) 他們正在讀英文。
>
> (C) 他們正在吃午餐。

答案 C

第二部份：問答

6. How are you doing these days?

(A) Nothing special.

(B) What day is today?

(C) I am studying.

> 最近過得如何？
>
> 選項：(A) 沒什麼特別的事。
>
> (B) 今天是星期幾？
>
> (C) 我正在讀書。

答案 A

7. How old are you?

(A) Eighteen.

(B) August.

(C) 1988.

> 你今年幾歲？
>
> 選項：(A) 十八歲。
>
> (B) 八月。
>
> (C) 一九八八年。

答案 A

8. Could you tell me where the children's books are?

(A) Sure. They're on the third floor.

(B) The gift shop is next to the coffee shop.

(C) I'm sorry. I didn't see any children here.

> 你能告訴我童書在哪裡嗎？
>
> 選項：(A) 當然。它們在三樓。
>
> (B) 禮物店在咖啡廳旁邊。
>
> (C) 很抱歉。我沒在這裡看到任何小孩子。

答案 A

9. I didn't sleep well last night.

(A) I need some sleep now.

(B) No wonder you look so tired.

(C) Thank you for buying me a cup of coffee.

> 我昨晚沒有睡好。
>
> 選項：(A) 我現在需要睡一下。
>
> (B) 難怪你看起來這麼累。
>
> (C) 謝謝你請我喝一杯咖啡。

答案 B

10. Mr. Lin's office. May I help you?

    (A) Yes. Can I see Mr. Lin today?

    (B) Yes. He is right there.

    (C) No, would you like to leave a message?

答案 A

林先生辦公室。我能為你效勞嗎？

選項：(A) 是。我今天能見林先生嗎？

      (B) 是的。他在那裡。

      (C) 不，你想要留言嗎？

11. Hi, Steve, would you like to go to the night market with us?

    (A) You are welcome.

    (B) Sure. It sounds like fun.

    (C) Don't mention it.

答案 B

嗨，史提夫，你願意跟我們去逛夜市嗎？

選項：(A) 不客氣。

      (B) 當然。那聽起來很有趣。

      (C) 別客氣。

12. Shall we try the steak?

    (A) Nice to meet you.

    (B) No, they're very happy.

    (C) Sure. Why not?

答案 C

我們應該試試看這塊牛排嗎？

選項：(A) 很高興認識你。

      (B) 不，他們很高興。

      (C) 好啊。有何不可？

13. I'm sorry for being late.

    (A) Thank you so much.

    (B) That's OK.

    (C) It's not my fault.

答案 B

很抱歉我遲到了。

選項：(A) 非常感謝你。

      (B) 沒關係。

      (C) 那不是我的錯。

14. I ordered an ice cream, but you brought me a cheesecake. I didn't order that.

    (A) Are you ready to order?

    (B) Oh, I'm sorry. I got it wrong.

    (C) There is no ice.

答案 B

我點了一份冰淇淋，不過你送來了一塊起司蛋糕。我並沒有點它。

選項：(A) 你準備好要點餐了嗎？

      (B) 噢，很抱歉。我弄錯了。

      (C) 這裡沒有冰。

15. When is the movie on?

    (A) There will be no one there.

    (B) On May 15.

電影是什麼時候上映？

選項：(A) 那裡一個都沒有。

      (B) 五月十五日。

(C) In the Lowe Theater.

(C) 在洛依戲院。

答案 B

第三部份：簡短對話

16. W: I can't stand my little sister. I don't want to share the room with her anymore.

    M: You look so angry. What did she do?

    W: She always messes up the room and never cleans it up.

    M: I understand. My little brother also does the same thing.

    Q: Who is the woman angry with?

    (A) Her little brother.

    (B) Her little sister.

    (C) Her little daughter.

女：我受不了我妹妹了。我不想再繼續跟她共用一間房間。

男：你看起來很生氣。她做了什麼？

女：她總是弄亂房間，卻從不打掃。

男：我懂。我弟弟也做一樣的事。

問題：這女生對誰生氣？

選項：(A) 她弟弟。

　　　(B) 她妹妹。

　　　(C) 她女兒。

答案 B

17. W: Hi, do you know what bus goes to the National Theater?

    M: Yes. You can take No. 212 or 307.

    W: When will the buses arrive?

    M: Less than ten minutes.

    Q: What does the woman ask the man?

    (A) Where to take the bus.

    (B) What bus stops at the National Theater.

    (C) How long the bus takes to the National Theater.

女：嗨，你知道哪一條路線的公車可以到國家劇院嗎？

男：知道。你可以搭乘 212 或 307。

女：公車什麼時候會到站？

男：不超過十分鐘。

問題：這女生向這男生詢問什麼？

選項：(A) 搭公車的地點。

　　　(B) 有停靠在國家劇院的公車。

　　　(C) 公車到國家劇院要花多久時間。

答案 B

18. M: Hi. Is there a Mr. Green living here?

    W: Yes. He's my father. May I ask who's calling?

男：嗨。請問格林先生住在這裡嗎？

女：是的。他是我父親。我可以請教您是哪一位？

M: Yes. This is Taipei Hospital calling. Your father had an accident but he is OK.

W: Oh, no. I'll be right there. Thank you very much.

Q: Where is Mr. Green?

    (A) He is in the hospital.

    (B) He is making a phone call.

    (C) He is at home.

男：當然。我們這裡是臺北醫院。你的父親出了一點意外，但他還好。

女：噢，天啊。我馬上趕過去。非常感謝你。

問題：格林先生現在在哪裡？

選項：(A) 他在醫院裡。

    (B) 他正在打電話。

    (C) 他在家。

答案 **A**

19. M: Have you ever been abroad?

W: Yeah. Japan, Canada, and the U.S. And how about you?

M: Just the U.S. I've always wanted to go to Japan, but never had a chance.

Q: How many countries has the man been to?

    (A) One.

    (B) Two.

    (C) Three.

男：你有出國過嗎？

女：有，日本、加拿大和美國。那你呢？

男：只有美國。我一直想去日本，但從未有機會。

問題：這男生去過幾個國家？

選項：(A) 一個。

    (B) 兩個。

    (C) 三個。

答案 **A**

20. M: Do you have time for a cup of coffee?

W: I'm afraid I can't. I have to see my dentist.

M: No problem. Some other time, then.

Q: Why does the woman refuse the man's invitation?

    (A) She doesn't like coffee.

    (B) She has to see her dentist.

    (C) She is afraid of the man.

男：你有時間來杯咖啡嗎？

女：恐怕不行。我必須看牙醫。

男：沒關係。那麼就下次吧。

問題：這女生為何拒絕這男生的邀請？

選項：(A) 她不喜歡咖啡。

    (B) 她必須去看牙醫。

    (C) 她怕這男生。

答案 **B**

21. W: What would you like to drink? Cold

女：你想喝什麼？冰啤酒？柳橙汁？

beer? Orange juice?

M: Thanks. But I think a glass of hot water will be fine.

W: Are you sure? Cold beer is your favorite.

M: I'd love to have it, but I caught a cold.

Q: What did the man prefer to drink?

   (A) Orange juice.

   (B) Cold beer.

   (C) Water.

男：謝了。不過我想來一杯熱水就可以了。

女：你確定嗎？冰啤酒是你的最愛。

男：我很想喝，但是我感冒了。

問題：這男生想要喝什麼？

選項：(A) 柳橙汁。

   (B) 冰啤酒。

   (C) 水。

答案 C

22. W: Hey, Ted. I lost the umbrella you lent me.

M: Oh, Mary. That was my favorite umbrella!

W: I'm really sorry about this. I will buy you a new one.

Q: Why did Mary apologize to Ted?

   (A) She lost Ted's umbrella.

   (B) She forgot to bring Ted's umbrella.

   (C) She didn't buy Ted a new umbrella.

女：嘿，泰德。我弄丟了你借我的雨傘。

男：噢，瑪莉。那是我最喜歡的雨傘耶！

女：關於這件事我真的很抱歉。我會買一把新的給你。

問題：瑪莉為什麼向泰德道歉？

選項：(A) 她把泰德的雨傘弄丟了。

   (B) 她忘了帶泰德的雨傘。

   (C) 她沒有買一把新的雨傘給泰德。

答案 A

23. W: Did you smell that?

M: What is it? Is something burning?

W: No. I think somebody is smoking.

M: But this is a non-smoking restaurant.

W: That's right. Let's speak to the manager.

Q: What was the woman complaining about?

女：你聞到了嗎？

男：是什麼？有東西燒焦了嗎？

女：不是。我覺得有人在抽菸。

男：但這是一間無菸餐廳。

女：沒錯。我們找經理說一下。

問題：這女生在抱怨什麼？

(A) The smell of burnt food.

(B) The smoke from a factory.

(C) The smoke in a non-smoking place.

答案 C

24. M: Why don't we try a new place this time?

W: Sure. Is it easy to get to?

M: Yes. It's not far from here, and I hear its seafood is very good.

Q: What are they talking about?

(A) A department store.

(B) A restaurant.

(C) A bookstore.

答案 B

25. M: So, which one is your daughter?

W: There. The girl dressed in red.

M: Oh, she is so cute. She has big eyes like yours.

W: Yes. She also has the same dark brown hair as mine.

Q: What is true about the woman's daughter?

(A) She has small eyes.

(B) She wears red clothes.

(C) Her hair color is light brown.

答案 B

第四部份：短文聽解

26. For question number 26, please look at the three pictures. Question number 26, listen to the following announcement.

選項：(A) 食物燒焦的味道。

(B) 來自工廠的煙味。

(C) 一個禁菸場所裡的菸味。

男：我們這次何不試試看去一個新地方？

女：好啊。可以很容易就到那邊嗎？

男：是的。它離這裡不遠，而且我聽說它的海鮮非常讚。

問題：他們在談論什麼？

選項：(A) 一間百貨公司。

(B) 一間餐廳。

(C) 一間書店。

男：那麼，哪一個是你的女兒？

女：在那裡。那個穿紅色衣服的女孩。

男：噢，她好可愛。她有像你一樣的大眼睛。

女：對啊，她也有和我一樣深棕色的頭髮。

問題：哪一個對於這女生的女兒的描述是正確的？

選項：(A) 她有小眼睛。

(B) 她穿紅色的衣服。

(C) 她的髮色是淺棕色。

第二十六題，請看這三張圖。第二十六題，注意聆聽接下來的廣播。梅在三點的時候最有可能去哪裡？

Where will May most probably go at 3?
Welcome to San Min Ocean Park. The dolphin show will start at 3 o'clock this afternoon and we look forward to seeing you at the pool.
(A) The library.
(B) The pool.
(C) The company.

答案 **B**

27. For question number 27, please look at the three pictures. Question number 27, listen to the following announcement. Where will you most probably hear this announcement?
Passengers to Hualien will be boarding on platform 3A. The train will be arriving in 1 minute. Thank you and wish you all a happy journey.
(A) On a train platform.
(B) In a bus station.
(C) On a train.

答案 **A**

28. For question number 28, please look at the three pictures. Question number 28, listen to the following message for David. Where did Tom go yesterday?
Hey, David. This is Tom. I want to tell you that I can't go to the movies with you today! I went to the beach yesterday, and I got a bad cold. I really need to take a rest. So, maybe next time. Bye.
(A) Went to a movie.

歡迎來到三民海洋公園。海豚秀將會在今天下午三點開始，我們期待在池畔見到您。

選項：(A) 圖書館。
　　　(B) 池畔。
　　　(C) 公司。

第二十七題，請看這三張圖。第二十七題，注意聆聽接下來的廣播。你最有可能在哪裡聽到這則廣播？

前往花蓮的旅客將在 3A 月臺上車。列車會在一分鐘後抵達。謝謝您，祝您旅途愉快。

選項：(A) 火車站的月臺上。
　　　(B) 公車站。
　　　(C) 火車上。

第二十八題，請看這三張圖。第二十八題，注意聆聽接下來給大衛的留言。湯姆昨天去哪裡？

嘿，大衛，我是湯姆。我想告訴你，我今天無法跟你去看電影了！我昨天去海邊然後得了重感冒。我真的需要好好的休息一下。那麼，或許下次吧。再見。

選項：(A) 看電影。

(B) Went jogging.

(C) Went to the beach.

答案 **C**

29. For question number 29, please look at the three pictures. Question number 29, listen to the following announcement. Where will you most probably hear this announcement?

Attention please. In the museum, please refrain from eating and drinking. In order to ensure the safety of all the exhibits, all forms of photography are not allowed. Thank you for your cooperation.

(A) In a jewelry shop.

(B) On the MRT.

(C) In a museum.

答案 **C**

30. For question number 30, please look at the three pictures. Question number 30, listen to the following short talk. What did Robert most likely do last night?

After finishing his homework, Robert felt a little hungry and tired. He wanted to buy something to eat. However, the moment he stepped out of the house, it started to rain. Therefore, he decided to go back home and go to sleep.

(A) Eat.

(B) Sleep.

(C) Cook.

答案 **B**

(B) 慢跑。

(C) 去海邊。

第二十九題，請看這三張圖。第二十九題，注意聆聽接下來的廣播。你最有可能在哪裡聽到這則廣播？

請注意。在這博物館裡，請不要飲食。為了確保展示品的安全，任何形式的攝影都是不允許的。謝謝您的合作。

選項：(A) 珠寶店裡。

(B) 捷運上。

(C) 博物館裡。

第三十題，請看這三張圖。第三十題，注意聆聽接下來的簡短談話。羅伯特昨晚最有可能做了什麼？

完成他的功課後，羅伯特覺得有一點飢餓和疲憊，他想去買東西吃。然而，當他踏出家後，外面開始下雨了。所以他決定回家睡覺。

選項：(A) 吃東西。

(B) 睡覺。

(C) 煮東西。

第一部份：看圖辨義

1. For question number 1, please look at picture A. Question number 1:

   Where are these people?

   (A) They are watching a movie.

   (B) They are in the movie theater.

   (C) They are sitting on the chairs.

   第一題，請看圖片 A。第一題：

   這些人在什麼地方？

   選項：(A) 他們在看電影。

   　　　(B) 他們在電影院裡。

   　　　(C) 他們坐在椅子上。

   答案　B

2. For question number 2, please look at picture B. Question number 2:

   What does the woman do?

   (A) She is a teacher.

   (B) She is a lawyer.

   (C) She is a nurse.

   第二題，請看圖片 B。第二題：

   這女生的職業是什麼？

   選項：(A) 她是一位老師。

   　　　(B) 她是一位律師。

   　　　(C) 她是一位護士。

   答案　C

3. For questions number 3 and 4, please look at picture C. Question number 3:

   What does this sign mean?

   (A) You are free to get one here.

   (B) You can get two but pay for one.

   (C) If you get one, the one is free.

   第三題及第四題，請看圖片 C。第三題：

   這個告示是什麼意思？

   選項：(A) 你能在這裡隨意拿一個。

   　　　(B) 你付一個的錢能拿兩個。

   　　　(C) 若你拿一個，它是免費的。

   答案　B

4. Question number 4, please look at picture C again.

   Where will this sign most likely be seen?

   (A) In a classroom.

   (B) In a gym.

   (C) In a supermarket.

   第四題，請再看一次圖片 C。

   最有可能在哪裡看到這個告示？

   選項：(A) 在一間教室裡。

   　　　(B) 在一間體育館裡。

   　　　(C) 在一間超級市場裡。

   答案　C

5. For question number 5, please look at picture D. Question number 5:
   Who is the man?
   (A) He is a basketball player.
   (B) He is a baseball player.
   (C) He is a football player.

   答案 A

第五題，請看圖片 D。第五題：

這男生是誰？
選項：(A) 他是一個籃球員。
　　　(B) 他是一個棒球員。
　　　(C) 他是一個美式足球員。

第二部份：問答

6. I want to thank you for your help.
   (A) Don't mention it.
   (B) I must apologize.
   (C) I wish I could.

   答案 A

我想謝謝你的幫忙。
選項：(A) 不客氣。
　　　(B) 我必須道歉。
　　　(C) 但願我可以。

7. When is your birthday?
   (A) 2005.
   (B) Summer.
   (C) July 4th.

   答案 C

你生日是什麼時候？
選項：(A) 二〇〇五年。
　　　(B) 夏天。
　　　(C) 七月四日。

8. I'm lost. Could you help me?
   (A) Yes. What would you like to order?
   (B) No, it's quite close.
   (C) Sure. Where do you want to go?

   答案 C

我迷路了。你能幫我嗎？
選項：(A) 是的。你想要點什麼？
　　　(B) 不，那很近。
　　　(C) 當然。你要去哪裡？

9. Would you mind opening the door for me?
   (A) No, not at all.
   (B) I may not go.
   (C) Don't do that.

   答案 A

你介意幫我開門嗎？

選項：(A) 不，一點也不介意。
　　　(B) 我可能不會去。
　　　(C) 別那樣做。

10. How do you like our new teacher?
    (A) Yes, I'm a teacher.

你覺得我們的新老師如何？
選項：(A) 是的，我是一個老師。

(B) I don't like him.

(C) I'll give you a hand.

答案 B

11. I have two tickets for the movie. Would you like to go with me?

(A) I'd like some tea, please.

(B) Sure. When will it be?

(C) How did you get the concert tickets?

我有兩張電影票。你要跟我一起去嗎？

選項：(A) 我想要一些茶，麻煩你。

(B) 好啊。什麼時候？

(C) 你是如何得到演奏會的票？

答案 B

12. Come on. Have another piece of pie.

(A) Sure. Here you are.

(B) You're welcome.

(C) No, thank you. I'm really full.

來吧。再來一片派。

選項：(A) 好。拿去。

(B) 不客氣。

(C) 不，謝了。我真的很飽。

答案 C

13. Why are you so late?

(A) All right, I'll go with you.

(B) I missed the train.

(C) You can save a lot of time.

你為什麼這麼晚才到？

選項：(A) 好吧，我跟你去。

(B) 我錯過了火車。

(C) 你可以節省很多時間。

答案 B

14. Could you bring some water for me?

(A) Sure, I'll be right back.

(B) Hot water will be fine.

(C) Coffee, please.

你可以給我一些水嗎？

選項：(A) 當然，我立刻就回來。

(B) 我要熱水。

(C) 我要咖啡，麻煩你。

答案 A

15. I'm tired of waiting for the bus.

(A) I usually walk to school.

(B) Me, too. Why don't we take a taxi?

(C) Yes, it's quite crowded on the bus.

我厭倦等公車了。

選項：(A) 我經常走路去學校。

(B) 我也是。何不搭計程車呢？

(C) 是的，公車上相當擁擠。

答案 B

第三部份：簡短對話

16. M: Excuse me. Does this bus go to the art museum?

W: You are going in the wrong direction. You should go to the other side of the road and take the bus in front of the supermarket.

M: I see. Thanks a lot.

Q: What will the man most likely do next?

(A) Cross over the road.

(B) Take this bus.

(C) Ask another person.

答案　**A**

男：不好意思。這輛公車會到美術館嗎？

女：你走錯方向了，你應該到對面，搭乘超級市場前的公車。

男：我知道了，謝謝你。

問題：這男生接下來最有可能做什麼？

選項：(A) 過馬路。

(B) 搭乘這輛公車。

(C) 詢問另一個人。

17. M: May I speak to Helen, please?

W: Oh, she just went out. Can I take a message?

M: Yes. Please ask her to call Fred. Thanks.

W: No problem. Let me write that down for you.

Q: What did the man want the woman to do?

(A) Ask Fred to come to the phone.

(B) Have Helen call Fred.

(C) Leave a message for Fred.

答案　**B**

男：我可以請海倫聽電話嗎？

女：噢，她剛出去。我能幫你留言嗎？

男：好。請她撥電話給佛瑞德。謝謝你。

女：沒問題，讓我幫你記下來。

問題：這男生要這女生做什麼？

選項：(A) 請佛瑞德來接電話。

(B) 請海倫打電話給佛瑞德。

(C) 留言給佛瑞德。

18. M: My father bought me a new computer yesterday.

W: Really? You're so lucky.

M: Yeah, now I can play my favorite game at home any time.

男：我爸爸昨天買了一臺新電腦給我。

女：真的嗎？你真是幸運。

男：是的，現在我可以隨時在家裡玩我喜歡的遊戲。

Q: What did the boy's father buy for him? | 問題：這男孩的爸爸買了什麼給他？
(A) A new car. | 選項：(A) 一輛新車。
(B) A new computer. | (B) 一臺新電腦。
(C) A new game. | (C) 一個新的遊戲。

答案 **B**

19. M: Can I see Mr. Lu tomorrow? | 男：我明天可以見盧先生嗎？
W: Let me see. How about 3 in the afternoon? | 女：我看看。下午三點鐘如何？
M: 3 o'clock will be fine. | 男：三點鐘這時間很好。
W: OK. If he finishes his work earlier, I'll let you know. | 女：好。如果他提早完成工作，我會告知你。
M: Thanks. | 男：謝謝。
Q: When will the man see Mr. Lu? | 問題：這男生什麼時候要見盧先生？
(A) This morning. | 選項：(A) 今天早上。
(B) This afternoon. | (B) 今天下午。
(C) Tomorrow afternoon. | (C) 明天下午。

答案 **C**

20. M: Hi, Lucy. Do you want to come to my party on Saturday night? | 男：嗨，露西。你要來參加我在星期六晚上辦的派對嗎？
W: This coming Saturday? | 女：這個星期六？
M: Yes. Are you free that night? | 男：是的。你那天晚上有空嗎？
W: Maria and I are going to a movie that night. Sorry. | 女：那天晚上我和瑪莉亞要去看電影。抱歉。
Q: What will Lucy do on Saturday night? | 問題：露西在星期六晚上將要做什麼？
(A) Go shopping. | 選項：(A) 購物。
(B) Go to a party. | (B) 參加派對。
(C) Go to a movie. | (C) 看電影。

答案 **C**

21. M: How about a piece of cheesecake? | 男：來一塊起司蛋糕如何？
W: Do they have anything else? | 女：還有沒有什麼其他的東西？
M: Well, how about strawberry cake? I tried it last time and it was good. | 男：那麼，草莓蛋糕怎麼樣？我上次吃過，很不錯。

W: That sounds great.

Q: What did the woman want?

   (A) A piece of strawberry cake.

   (B) A piece of cheesecake.

   (C) Nothing.

答案 **A**

22. W: Wow, what a beautiful cat!

M: Look at its eyes. Cats are so smart. They seem to understand what you are saying.

W: I really like to have one.

Q: What are they talking about?

   (A) Games.

   (B) Pets.

   (C) Books.

答案 **B**

23. M: I am tired of my job.

W: What's wrong with your job?

M: I sit in front of the computer all day long. All I do is typing.

W: That doesn't sound too good. Maybe you should change your job.

Q: What does the woman suggest?

   (A) The man should stop complaining.

   (B) The man should quit his job.

   (C) The man should do some exercise.

答案 **B**

24. W: So, what do you think of my new apartment?

M: I like it. This is just the perfect place for you.

女：聽起來不錯。

問題：這女生要什麼？

選項：(A) 一塊草莓蛋糕。

      (B) 一塊起司蛋糕。

      (C) 什麼都不要。

女：哇，好漂亮的貓咪！

男：你看牠的眼睛。貓很聰明。牠們看起來似乎懂得你在說什麼。

女：我真的好想有一隻貓。

問題：他們在談論什麼？

選項：(A) 遊戲。

      (B) 寵物。

      (C) 書籍。

男：我厭倦了我的工作。

女：你的工作怎麼了？

男：我整天都坐在電腦前，不停地打字。

女：聽起來不太好。或許你該換工作了。

問題：這女生建議什麼？

選項：(A) 這男生應該停止抱怨。

      (B) 這男生應該辭職。

      (C) 這男生應該做些運動。

女：那麼，你覺得我的新公寓如何？

男：我喜歡。這是最適合你的地方。

W: Thanks. Could you help me move this Sunday?

M: Sure. Why not?

Q: What will the man do on Sunday?

   (A) Move to a new apartment.

   (B) Do a favor for the woman.

   (C) Stay at home.

女：謝了。這個星期天你能幫我搬家嗎？

男：當然，為什麼不呢？

問題：這男生星期天將要做什麼？

選項：(A) 搬到新公寓。

      (B) 幫這女生一個忙。

      (C) 待在家裡。

答案　**B**

25. W: Where is your wife?

M: She's over there in a white dress.

W: Oh! She looks nice in white.

Q: What are these people mainly discussing?

   (A) A white dress.

   (B) The man's wife.

   (C) The woman's looks.

女：你太太在哪裡？

男：她在那邊，穿著白色套裝。

女：噢！她穿白色看起來很不錯。

問題：說話者主要在討論什麼？

選項：(A) 一件白色套裝。

      (B) 這男生的太太。

      (C) 這女生的美貌。

答案　**B**

第四部份：短文聽解

26. For question number 26, please look at the three pictures. Question number 26, Kelly wants to give her dad a birthday gift. What will Kelly most probably buy? My dad's birthday is coming. I want to buy him a new cell phone as a birthday present. But his bike was stolen yesterday. He cycles to work every day. I think it is a better idea to buy him a new bike.

   (A) A bike.

   (B) A cell phone.

   (C) A car.

第二十六題，請看這三張圖。第二十六題，凱莉想要給她父親一個生日禮物。凱莉最有可能買什麼？

我爸爸的生日快到了。我想要買一支新手機當成生日禮物給他。但是他的腳踏車昨天被偷了。他每天都騎腳踏車去上班。我想買腳踏車給他是個較好的點子。

選項：(A) 腳踏車。

      (B) 手機。

      (C) 汽車。

答案　**A**

27. For question number 27, please look at the three pictures. Question number 27, Dan is looking for a book. Where will Dan go today?

Dan loves to read, so he went to a book fair with his friends last Sunday. Yet, he didn't find his favorite writer's new book. Therefore, he plans to go to the bookstore today to see if he can find the book.

(A) The post office.

(B) The fast food restaurant.

(C) The bookstore.

答案 C

28. For question number 28, please look at the three pictures. Question number 28, listen to the following announcement. Where will you most probably hear this announcement?

Ladies and gentlemen, this is your captain speaking. We will be arriving at Taoyuan International Airport in 30 minutes. Our flying altitude is 12,000 feet. The local time is 8:15 a.m. Thank you for flying with us, and we hope we will have the chance to serve you again.

(A) On a plane.

(B) On a bus.

(C) On a train.

答案 A

29. For question number 29, please look at the three pictures. Question number 29,

第二十七題，請看這三張圖。第二十七題，丹正在找一本書。丹今天將會去哪裡？

丹熱愛閱讀，所以他上星期天跟朋友去了書展。但是他沒有找到他最喜愛的作者的新書。因此，他打算今天去書店，看他是否能找到那本書。

選項：(A) 郵局。

(B) 速食店。

(C) 書店。

第二十八題，請看這三張圖。第二十八題，注意聆聽接下來的廣播。你最有可能在哪裡聽到這則廣播？

各位先生女士，這是機長廣播。我們將在三十分鐘內抵達桃園國際機場。我們現在的飛行高度是一萬兩千英尺。當地時間為上午八點十五分。感謝您搭乘本班機，希望我們能有機會再次的為您服務。

選項：(A) 飛機上。

(B) 公車上。

(C) 火車上。

第二十九題，請看這三張圖。第二十九題，注意聆聽接下來的簡短談話。

listen to the following short talk. What transportation will Matthew choose to meet Jenny on time?

Matthew is almost late for the appointment with Jenny. He thinks waiting for the bus is a waste of time and the nearest MRT station is far from his home. Therefore, he decides to ride a motorcycle to meet Jenny.

(A) A motorcycle.

(B) The MRT.

(C) A bus.

答案 **A**

30. For question number 30, please look at the three pictures. Question number 30, listen to the following short talk. Where was Miranda?

Miranda went mountain climbing with her family yesterday. The air there was really fresh and cool. From the top, she had a good view of the city. Everything below looked so small.

(A) On the roof.

(B) On the balcony.

(C) On the top of the mountain.

答案 **C**

為了準時與珍妮碰面，馬修會選擇什麼交通工具？

跟珍妮的約會馬修快遲到了。他認為等公車很浪費時間而最近的捷運站又離他家很遠。所以，他決定騎摩托車去見珍妮。

選項：(A) 摩托車。
　　　(B) 捷運。
　　　(C) 公車。

第三十題，請看這三張圖。第三十題，注意聆聽接下來的簡短談話。米蘭達在哪裡？

米蘭達昨天和家人去爬山。那裡的空氣新鮮又冰冷。在山頂，城市的景色盡收眼底。所有的東西看起來都好小。

選項：(A) 在屋頂。
　　　(B) 在陽臺。
　　　(C) 在山頂。

第一部份：看圖辨義

1. For question number 1, please look at picture A. Question number 1:

   What does the boy want to eat?

   (A) Chinese food.

   (B) Seafood.

   (C) Fast food.

第一題，請看圖片 A。第一題：

這男孩想要吃什麼？

選項：(A) 中式餐點。

(B) 海鮮。

(C) 速食。

答案 **C**

2. For question number 2, please look at picture B. Question number 2:

   What do you see in the picture?

   (A) Some dirty dishes.

   (B) Some forks and knives.

   (C) Some clean plates.

第二題，請看圖片 B。第二題：

你在這張圖中看到什麼？

選項：(A) 一些髒盤子。

(B) 一些叉子和刀子。

(C) 一些乾淨的盤子。

答案 **A**

3. For question number 3, please look at picture C. Question number 3:

   Who might be interested in this shop?

   (A) Someone who loves dogs.

   (B) Someone who likes to eat vegetables.

   (C) Someone who wants to buy dresses.

第三題，請看圖片 C。第三題：

誰可能對這家店有興趣？

選項：(A) 愛狗人士。

(B) 喜歡吃蔬菜的人。

(C) 想買套裝的人。

答案 **C**

4. For question number 4, please look at picture D. Question number 4:

   Where are the two people?

   (A) They are at a bus stop.

   (B) They are in a restaurant.

   (C) They are at a train station.

第四題，請看圖片 D。第四題：

這兩個人在什麼地方？

選項：(A) 他們在公車站。

(B) 他們在餐廳裡。

(C) 他們在火車站。

答案 **C**

5. For question number 5, please look at

第五題，請看圖片 E。第五題：

picture E. Question number 5:

What does the sign mean?

(A) You don't have to write down the address.

(B) You don't have to stamp the letter.

(C) You have to pay the U.S. postage.

這個告示是什麼意思？

選項：(A) 你不需要寫地址。

(B) 你不需要在信件上貼郵票。

(C) 你必須付美國郵資。

答案　**B**

第二部份：問答

6. Have you ever been to Taiwan?

(A) Really? I thought Taiwan is a small island.

(B) I've never been abroad.

(C) I don't like Taiwanese food.

你曾經去過臺灣嗎？

選項：(A) 真的嗎？我以為臺灣是個小島。

(B) 我從未出國過。

(C) 我不喜歡臺灣的食物。

答案　**B**

7. Where is the train station?

(A) It is around the corner.

(B) It is going to be on time.

(C) The station closes at 11 p.m.

火車站在什麼地方？

選項：(A) 就在轉角處。

(B) 它會準時到。

(C) 車站在晚上十一點關門。

答案　**A**

8. Hi. Is Rex there?

(A) No, thanks.

(B) No, I don't.

(C) Sorry. He is not in.

嗨。雷克斯在嗎？

選項：(A) 不，謝了。

(B) 不，我不要。

(C) 抱歉。他不在。

答案　**C**

9. I wonder if I could use your telephone.

(A) I wonder how.

(B) It is useful.

(C) Of course.

我想問是否可以使用你的電話。

選項：(A) 我想知道要怎麼做。

(B) 它很有用。

(C) 當然。

答案　**C**

10. How do you feel today?

(A) Much better.

你今天覺得如何？

選項：(A) 好多了。

(B) No, it won't help.

(C) I can tell you why.

(B) 不，那沒用。

(C) 我可以告訴你為什麼。

11. Do you want to go to Sam's party on Sunday?

(A) Thanks for your help.

(B) I was tired last Sunday.

(C) Yes. What time?

星期日你要去參加山姆的派對嗎？

選項：(A) 謝謝你的幫忙。

(B) 上星期日我很累。

(C) 好啊。什麼時候？

12. Thank you for taking me downtown.

(A) Thanks a million.

(B) It's my pleasure.

(C) How kind of you.

謝謝你帶我到市區。

選項：(A) 非常感謝。

(B) 這是我的榮幸。

(C) 你真好。

13. Hey, your music is too loud.

(A) Sorry. I'll turn it down right away.

(B) He is not a musician.

(C) Yes. You are welcome.

嘿，你的音樂太大聲了。

選項：(A) 抱歉。我馬上把音量調低。

(B) 他並不是音樂家。

(C) 是的。不客氣。

14. Please clean your room at least once a week!

(A) The work is wonderful.

(B) Thanks a lot.

(C) OK. I'll do that.

請至少每星期清理一次你的房間！

選項：(A) 這工作太棒了。

(B) 非常感謝。

(C) 好。我會照做。

15. How do you like my new shoes?

(A) I think they look great.

(B) They are size 12.

(C) I bought them for my mother.

你喜歡我的新鞋嗎？

選項：(A) 我覺得它們看起來很不錯。

(B) 它們的尺寸是十二號。

(C) 我買給我媽媽。

第三部份：簡短對話

16. M: How many people are there in your family?

   W: My family is small. There are only three people. How about you?

   M: There are seven people in my family, my parents, an elder brother, three younger sisters, and me.

   W: Wow, what a large family!

   Q: How many people are there in their families in total?

      (A) Twelve.

      (B) Ten.

      (C) Eight.

男：你的家庭有幾個人呢？

女：我的家庭很小，只有三個人。你呢？

男：我家有七個人，我父母、一個哥哥、三個妹妹、還有我。

女：哇，真是個大家庭！

問題：他們的家庭一共有幾個人？

選項：(A) 十二個。

     (B) 十個。

     (C) 八個。

答案　**B**

17. M: San Min Airline, may I help you?

   W: Yes, I would like to book two tickets from Taipei to Tokyo.

   M: On what date would you like to leave?

   W: October 6th, is there any morning flight?

   Q: What will the man most likely do next?

      (A) Check the flight schedule for her.

      (B) Fly to Tokyo on October 6th.

      (C) Book two bus tickets to Taipei.

男：三民航空，請問能幫你什麼嗎？

女：是的，我想訂兩張從臺北到東京的機票。

男：你幾號想離開呢？

女：十月六日，有早晨的班機嗎？

問題：這男生接下來最有可能做什麼？

選項：(A) 幫她確認航班時刻表。

     (B) 於十月六日飛往東京。

     (C) 訂兩張往臺北的公車票。

答案　**A**

18. W: Big Tree Café. May I help you?

   M: Yes. Do you have any tables available for tonight?

女：大樹咖啡。有什麼我可以效勞的嗎？

男：是的。你們今晚有空位嗎？

W: Certainly. For how many people?	女：當然。幾位呢？
M: 8.	男：八位。
Q: When will the man go to Big Tree Café?	問題：這男生將於什麼時候到大樹咖啡用餐？
(A) Tonight.	選項：(A) 今晚。
(B) 8 o'clock.	(B) 八點。
(C) Next month.	(C) 下個月。

答案　**A**

19. M: What's the matter with you?	男：你怎麼了？
W: I've had a sore throat for days and I feel even worse today. I have a temperature.	女：我已經喉嚨痛了好幾天，今天覺得更不舒服，我發燒了。
M: Well, drinking lots of water and taking a rest will help.	男：那麼，多喝水和休息一下將會有幫助。
W: I think I have the flu and need to take medicine. Can you drive me to the hospital?	女：我想我得了流行性感冒，而且需要吃藥。你能開車載我去醫院嗎？
Q: What's wrong with the woman?	問題：這女生哪裡不對勁？
(A) Her nose is running.	選項：(A) 她在流鼻水。
(B) She has a fever.	(B) 她發燒了。
(C) She wants to drive.	(C) 她想要開車。

答案　**B**

20. W: Hey, Tom. Do you want to go for a ride with me on Saturday?	女：嘿，湯姆。星期六你要跟我去兜風嗎？
M: I'd like to, but there's a problem.	男：我很想，不過有個問題。
W: What is it?	女：是什麼？
M: Oh, I promised Chuck I'd go to a movie with him.	男：噢，我答應查克要和他去看電影。
Q: What will Tom do on Saturday?	問題：湯姆星期六將要做什麼？
(A) He's going to solve a problem.	選項：(A) 他將要解決問題。
(B) He and Chuck are going to a movie.	(B) 他和查克將要去看電影。

(C) He is going to a party.

(C) 他將要去參加派對。

答案 B

21. W: Would you like some Chinese food for dinner?

M: No, we had it yesterday. How about Korean food?

W: That sounds like a good idea.

M: Great. I know an excellent Korean restaurant. Follow me!

Q: What did the man eat yesterday?

(A) Chinese food.

(B) Japanese food.

(C) Korean food.

女：晚餐你想吃中式料理嗎？

男：不要，我們昨天吃過了。吃韓式料理如何？

女：聽起來是個不錯的主意。

男：太好了。我知道一間很棒的韓式餐廳，跟我來！

問題：這男生昨天晚餐吃什麼？

選項：(A) 中式料理。

(B) 日式料理。

(C) 韓式料理。

答案 A

22. W: I'm sorry! I lost the book you lent me last week.

M: What? Where did you lose it?

W: I really don't know. I'll buy a new one for you.

M: No. Never mind. Just be careful next time.

Q: What are the speakers mainly discussing?

(A) Where to buy a new book.

(B) How to make it up to the man.

(C) When to apologize for the mistake.

女：很抱歉！你上星期借我的書，我弄丟了。

男：什麼？你在哪裡弄丟的？

女：我真的不知道。我會買一本新的還你。

男：不了，沒關係，下次小心一點就好。

問題：說話者主要在討論什麼？

選項：(A) 去哪裡買本新書。

(B) 如何補償這男生。

(C) 何時該為這個錯誤道歉。

答案 B

23. W: Jack, I didn't see your report on my desk.

M: I'm sorry. I left it at home. Could I hand it in tomorrow?

女：傑克，我在桌上沒看到你的報告。

男：抱歉。我把它忘在家裡了。我可以明天再交嗎？

W: All right. But don't let it happen again.

女：好吧。不過別再發生這種事。

Q: What happened to Jack's report?

問題：傑克的報告怎麼了？

    (A) It was lost on the bus.

選項：(A) 它掉在公車上。

    (B) It was left at home.

        (B) 它被忘在家裡。

    (C) It was on the teacher's desk.

        (C) 它在老師桌上。

答案 **B**

24. W: You look great in that T-shirt.

女：你穿那件 T 恤很好看。

M: Thanks. I'm glad you like it.

男：謝了。我很高興你喜歡。

W: Where did you get it? I'd like to buy one, too.

女：你從哪裡弄來的？我也想買一件。

M: I bought it at San Min Department Store. It's on sale now.

男：我在三民百貨公司買的，它現在特價中。

Q: What are the speakers talking about?

問題：說話者在談論什麼？

    (A) Clothes.

選項：(A) 衣服。

    (B) Exercise.

        (B) 運動。

    (C) Food.

        (C) 食物。

答案 **A**

25. M: Hi, I'd like to return this coat.

男：嗨，我想退還這件外套。

W: What's the problem?

女：有什麼問題？

M: Look, it's too small for me.

男：你看，它對我而言太小件了。

Q: Why did the man want to return the coat?

問題：這男生為什麼要退還外套？

    (A) The coat is too expensive.

選項：(A) 這外套太貴了。

    (B) The size is not right.

        (B) 尺寸不對。

    (C) The color is wrong.

        (C) 顏色不對。

答案 **B**

第四部份：短文聽解

26. For question number 26, please look at the three pictures. Question number 26, listen to the following short talk. What will Justin most likely do next?

第二十六題，請看這三張圖。第二十六題，注意聆聽接下來的簡短談話。賈斯汀接下來最有可能做什麼？

Justin wants to buy a notebook. The shop owner says he can give Justin a discount if he pays in cash, but Justin is just out of cash. He has to go to the ATM.
(A) Go jogging.
(B) Order a meal.
(C) Withdraw money from an ATM.

賈斯汀想要買一臺筆記型電腦。老闆說如果賈斯汀付現金的話他能給一點折扣，但是賈斯汀的現金用完了。他必須到提款機。
選項：(A) 慢跑。
(B) 點餐。
(C) 在提款機領錢。

答案　**C**

27. For question number 27, please look at the three pictures. Question number 27, Linda is leaving a phone message for Chris. What will Chris most likely do next?
Hi, Chris, this is Linda. I have to pick my parents up from the airport now. Therefore, I don't have time to cook dinner. But I had made a reservation at our favorite restaurant at 7 o'clock. I would like you to meet my parents tonight. Please be there on time.
(A) Have dinner with Linda's parents.
(B) Pick Linda's parents up from the airport.
(C) Cook Linda's parents a good dinner.

第二十七題，請看這三張圖。第二十七題，琳達正在留語音訊息給克里斯。克里斯接下來最有可能做什麼？

嗨，克里斯，我是琳達。我現在必須去機場接我的父母。所以我沒有時間煮晚餐，但是我已經在我們最喜歡的餐廳訂了七點的位子。我希望你跟我的父母見面。請準時出席。

選項：(A) 與琳達父母共進晚餐。
(B) 去機場接琳達父母。
(C) 為琳達父母煮豐盛的晚餐。

答案　**A**

28. For question number 28, please look at the three pictures. Question number 28, listen to the following announcement. Where will you most probably hear it?
There is an engine problem with the plane, so flight SQ877 will be delayed. We are truly sorry for the delay. We

第二十八題，請看這三張圖。第二十八題，注意聆聽接下來的廣播。你最有可能在哪裡聽到這則廣播？

班機 SQ877 因為引擎發生問題將會延誤。我們對於班機的延誤深感抱歉。我們將會盡快的通知您新的登機時

will inform you of the new boarding time as soon as possible. Thank you for your cooperation and patience.

(A) In a library.

(B) At an airport.

(C) In a bookstore.

答案　**B**

29. For question number 29, please look at the three pictures. Question number 29, listen to the following short talk. Where will Alicia meet her friend?

Excuse me. I think I got lost. Do you know how to get to 2nd street? I have to meet my friend in a movie theater at 9 o'clock and I'm almost late.

(A) The bank.

(B) The movie theater.

(C) On 2nd street.

答案　**B**

30. For question number 30, please look at the three pictures. Question number 30, listen to the following short talk. What will Lucas most probably do?

The weather is hot. Lucas is playing basketball with his friends and sweating heavily. He feels so uncomfortable and can't wait to take a shower right away.

(A) Take a shower.

(B) Play basketball.

(C) Wash his car.

答案　**A**

間。謝謝您的合作與耐心。

選項：(A) 圖書館。

(B) 機場。

(C) 書店。

第二十九題，請看這三張圖。第二十九題，注意聆聽接下來的簡短談話。艾莉西亞跟她的朋友將在哪裡碰面？

不好意思。我想我迷路了。你知道如何到第二街嗎？我在九點時要跟我的朋友在一家電影院碰面而且我快遲到了。

選項：(A) 銀行。

(B) 電影院。

(C) 第二街。

第三十題，請看這三張圖。第三十題，注意聆聽接下來的簡短談話。盧卡斯最有可能做什麼？

天氣很炎熱。盧卡斯正在跟他的朋友打籃球，流了很多汗。他覺得很不舒服並且迫不及待的想要立刻沖澡。

選項：(A) 沖澡。

(B) 打籃球。

(C) 洗車。

第一部份：看圖辨義

1. For questions number 1 and 2, please look at picture A. Question number 1: What is true about the map?

   (A) The bus stop is next to the city park.

   (B) The man is standing in front of the city park.

   (C) The bus stop and the city park are in different directions.

第一題及第二題，請看圖片 A。第一題：

哪一個關於地圖的敘述是正確的？

選項：(A) 公車站在城市公園旁邊。

(B) 這男生站在城市公園的前面。

(C) 公車站和城市公園在不同的方向。

答案 **C**

2. Question number 2, please look at picture A again. Which way should the man go to get to the bus stop?

   (A) Go straight.

   (B) Go straight and turn left.

   (C) Go straight and turn right.

第二題，請再看一次圖片 A。這男生該往哪個方向以到達公車站？

選項：(A) 直走。

(B) 直走後，左轉。

(C) 直走後，右轉。

答案 **C**

3. For questions number 3 and 4, please look at picture B. Question number 3: What does this advertisement mean?

   (A) The shop offers special items at a lower price every week.

   (B) Forty percent of the cameras in the store are on sale.

   (C) The shop offers a forty percent discount on all cameras.

第三題及第四題，請看圖片 B。第三題：

這個廣告是什麼意思？

選項：(A) 店家每週提供較低價的特殊商品。

(B) 店裡有百分之四十的相機都在打折。

(C) 店家的所有相機都有百分之四十的折扣。

答案 **A**

4. Question number 4, please look at picture B again. Who might be interested in this advertisement?

第四題，請再看一次圖片 B。誰可能對這個廣告有興趣？

(A) Painters.

(B) Photographers.

(C) Singers.

選項：(A) 畫家。

(B) 攝影師。

(C) 歌手。

答案 **B**

5. For question number 5, please look at picture C. Question number 5:

What is the woman doing?

(A) Watching television.

(B) Using a hair dryer.

(C) Playing computer games.

第五題，請看圖片 C。第五題：

這女生在做什麼？

選項：(A) 看電視。

(B) 使用吹風機。

(C) 玩電腦遊戲。

答案 **B**

第二部份：問答

6. Do you have any brothers or sisters?

(A) Yes. My father is a doctor.

(B) No. I am an only child.

(C) Yes. My brother and sister are students, too.

你有任何兄弟姊妹嗎？

選項：(A) 是的。我父親是一個醫生。

(B) 沒有。我是獨生子。

(C) 是的。我的兄弟姊妹也都是學生。

答案 **B**

7. Who will take you to the airport?

(A) My father will.

(B) It's 2:30 p.m.

(C) I'm going to Japan.

誰會帶你到機場？

選項：(A) 我爸爸。

(B) 下午兩點三十分。

(C) 我將要去日本。

答案 **A**

8. Do you want to leave a message?

(A) I'm not leaving.

(B) Yes. Please tell her Mary called.

(C) Thanks for calling.

你想要留言嗎？

選項：(A) 我沒打算離開。

(B) 是。請告訴她瑪莉來電。

(C) 謝謝您來電。

答案 **B**

9. Would you dance with me?

(A) You're welcome.

(B) Sure. Here you are.

你願意跟我跳舞嗎？

選項：(A) 不客氣。

(B) 當然。拿去吧。

(C) I'd love to.

10. I need to see Dr. Winston. When will be the best time?

　　(A) I had a great time last night.

　　(B) How about tomorrow morning around 10?

　　(C) I'm sorry. He is my father.

11. Sara, do you want to go shopping with me?

　　(A) No, thanks. I have work to do.

　　(B) I'm sorry. I'm new in town.

　　(C) Yes, this is my shop.

12. When will the show start?

　　(A) Park Theater.

　　(B) In 15 minutes.

　　(C) I like it.

13. A hamburger and a medium coke, please.

　　(A) How much is it?

　　(B) Where is my coke?

　　(C) For here or to go?

14. Excuse me, I didn't order a steak.

　　(A) Sorry, I'll change it for you.

　　(B) Sorry, it is out of order.

　　(C) Sorry, the place is closed.

(C) 我很樂意。

我要見溫斯頓醫生。什麼時候最適合？

選項：(A) 我昨天晚上玩得很開心。

　　　(B) 明天早上大約十點左右如何？

　　　(C) 很抱歉。他是我爸爸。

莎拉，你要跟我去逛街購物嗎？

選項：(A) 不，謝了。我有工作要做。

　　　(B) 很抱歉。我剛來這個地方。

　　　(C) 是的，這是我的店。

表演什麼時候開始？

選項：(A) 公園劇院。

　　　(B) 在十五分鐘內。

　　　(C) 我喜歡。

麻煩你，一個漢堡跟中杯可樂。

選項：(A) 它多少錢？

　　　(B) 我的可樂在哪裡？

　　　(C) 這裡用或外帶？

不好意思，我沒有點這份牛排。

選項：(A) 抱歉，我幫你換。

　　　(B) 抱歉，它故障了。

　　　(C) 抱歉，已經打烊了。

15. Your house is so beautiful.
    (A) All right, I'll do that.
    (B) You did a great job. Keep going.
    (C) Thanks. I'm so happy to hear that.

答案 **C**

你的房子好漂亮。
選項：(A) 好的，我會做。
    (B) 做得好。繼續下去。
    (C) 謝謝。很高興聽你這樣說。

第三部份：簡短對話

16. W: This is a good book. You should read it, too.

    M: What type of book is it?

    W: It's a crime novel.

    M: Oh, I like crime ones. I'll read it when I'm free.

    Q: What are these people mainly discussing?

    (A) A crime.
    (B) A book.
    (C) A drama.

答案 **B**

女：這是一本好書。你也應該讀它。

男：是什麼類型的書？

女：它是一本犯罪小說。

男：哦，我喜歡犯罪小說。當我有空的時候，我會讀的。

問題：說話者主要在討論什麼？

選項：(A) 一個犯罪行為。
    (B) 一本書。
    (C) 一齣戲劇。

17. M: Hi, is there a Spring Movie Theater near here?

    W: I'm sorry. I don't know where it is.

    M: Oh, that's OK. Thanks anyway.

    Q: What will the man probably do next?

    (A) Take the woman to the movie theater.
    (B) Ask somebody else.
    (C) Show the woman his movie ticket.

答案 **B**

男：嗨，這附近有沒有一間春天戲院？

女：很抱歉。我不知道它在哪裡。

男：噢，沒關係。不過還是謝謝你。

問題：這男生接下來可能會做什麼？

選項：(A) 帶這女生到戲院。

    (B) 問別人。
    (C) 把電影票展示給這女生看。

18. W: I'm sorry. James just went out for lunch. He will be back at 2 o'clock.

女：很抱歉。詹姆士剛剛出去吃午餐了。他兩點才會回來。

M: Well, could you tell him our baseball practice will start at 3 tomorrow?

W: Sure, no problem.

Q: When does this conversation most likely take place?

(A) 12 o'clock.

(B) 2 o'clock.

(C) 3 o'clock.

男：那麼，你能不能告訴他，我們的棒球練習將於明天三點開始？

女：當然。沒問題。

問題：這個對話最有可能發生在什麼時候？

選項：(A) 十二點。

(B) 兩點。

(C) 三點。

答案 A

19. M: How do you like this dress?

W: Well, I don't think I look too good in red. Do you have darker colors for this dress?

M: I am sorry, ma'am. Red is the only color of this dress.

W: OK. I'll try something else.

Q: Why didn't the woman want the dress?

(A) She didn't like the size.

(B) She didn't like the color.

(C) She didn't like the style.

男：你覺得這件套裝如何？

女：嗯，我覺得我穿紅色不怎麼好看。這件套裝有其他比較深的顏色嗎？

男：我很抱歉，太太。這件套裝只有紅色。

女：好。我會再試試看別的。

問題：這女生為何不要這件套裝？

選項：(A) 她不喜歡它的尺寸。

(B) 她不喜歡它的顏色。

(C) 她不喜歡它的款式。

答案 B

20. M: Hi, Maggie. Would you like to go to the movie "Spider Man" with me on Friday night?

W: What time?

M: 7:30.

W: I can't make it. I will be in a Japanese class until 8.

Q: Why will Maggie NOT go to the movie with the man?

(A) She doesn't like the movie.

男：嗨，瑪姬。星期五晚上你願意跟我去看電影「蜘蛛人」嗎？

女：什麼時候？

男：七點半。

女：我趕不上。我將會上日文課到八點。

問題：瑪姬為什麼不跟這男生去看電影？

選項：(A) 她不喜歡這部電影。

(B) She is a Japanese.

(C) She will be in class.

21. M: Hey, you should try the fried shrimps.

W: I don't know. Fried food is not good for health.

M: I know. But once in a while should be OK.

W: All right, I'll have some.

Q: Where are these two people?

　(A) They are friends.

　(B) Shrimps are good.

　(C) In a restaurant.

22. W: Hey, Johnny. Where were you last night?

M: I was out with Lucy. Why?

W: You promised to join us at the KTV for my birthday. Remember?

M: Oh, no. I'm really sorry. I forgot.

Q: What did the man do last night?

　(A) He went out with Lucy.

　(B) He went to the KTV.

　(C) He went to a birthday party.

23. M: Helen, please collect the homework from the class for me.

W: Sure. Sir, may I ask Mary to help me?

M: Of course. Oh, don't forget to put it on my office desk.

(B) 她是一個日本人。

(C) 她將會在上課。

男：嘿，你應該試試看這個炸蝦。

女：我不知道。油炸食物對健康不好。

男：我知道。不過偶一為之應該還好。

女：好吧，我吃一點。

問題：這兩個人在什麼地方？

選項：(A) 他們是朋友。

　　　(B) 蝦子很好吃。

　　　(C) 在餐廳裡。

女：嘿，強尼。你昨晚在哪裡？

男：我跟露西出去。為什麼這樣問？

女：你答應要跟我們到 KTV 參加我的生日。記得嗎？

男：噢，不。我真的很抱歉。我忘了。

問題：這男生昨晚做什麼？

選項：(A) 他跟露西出去。

　　　(B) 他去 KTV。

　　　(C) 他去參加生日宴會。

男：海倫，請幫我跟全班收取家庭作業。

女：好。老師，我可以請瑪莉幫忙嗎？

男：當然。哦，別忘了把作業放在我的辦公桌上。

W: OK. See you next class.

Q: Who are these speakers?

    (A) A teacher and a student.

    (B) A boss and a worker.

    (C) A customer and a waitress.

女：好，下節課見。

問題：這些說話者是誰？

選項：(A) 一位老師與一位學生。

    (B) 一位上司與一位員工。

    (C) 一位顧客與一位女服務生。

答案 A

24. W: Tickets for two adults, please.

    M: Would you like a bag of popcorn and a Coke? It only costs extra $50.

    W: No, thank you. That's all.

    M: OK then. That would be $560.

    Q: How much are the tickets?

        (A) 50 dollars.

        (B) 610 dollars.

        (C) 560 dollars.

女：請給我兩張成人票。

男：你要一袋爆米花和可樂嗎？只需多花 50 元。

女：不了，謝謝。這樣就好。

男：好，那麼一共是 560 元。

問題：票價是多少？

選項：(A) 50 元。

    (B) 610 元。

    (C) 560 元。

答案 C

25. W: Hi, I bought a desk lamp here yesterday.

    M: Yes. How may I help you?

    W: I want to return it because it's not working.

    Q: Where are the speakers?

        (A) In a classroom.

        (B) In a store.

        (C) At home.

女：嗨，我昨天在這裡買了一臺桌燈。

男：是的。有什麼我可效勞的嗎？

女：我要退還它，因為無法作用。

問題：這些說話者在什麼地方？

選項：(A) 在教室裡。

    (B) 在商店裡。

    (C) 在家裡。

答案 B

第四部份：短文聽解

26. For question number 26, please look at the three pictures. Question number 26, Sandra left a message on the answering machine. Where will Sandra most probably go?

第二十六題，請看這三張圖。第二十六題，珊卓拉在答錄機裡留了一個留言。珊卓拉最有可能去哪裡？

Hey, Mom. It's me, Sandra. I'm at Lisa's house now. We will eat dinner in an Italian restaurant. I won't be home till 11 o'clock. Don't wait up for me. Bye.

(A) Lisa's house.

(B) Italian restaurant.

(C) Amusement park.

嘿！媽，我是珊卓拉。我現在在麗莎家。我們將會到一家義大利餐廳吃晚餐。我到十一點才會回去，別等門。再見。

選項：(A) 麗莎家。

(B) 義式餐廳。

(C) 遊樂園。

答案 B

27. For question number 27, please look at the three pictures. Question number 27, listen to the following announcement. Where will you most probably hear this announcement?

Ladies and gentlemen, this is your captain speaking. We will be passing through some turbulence. For your own safety, please return to your seat immediately and fasten your seat belt. Thank you for your cooperation.

(A) On the plane.

(B) On an airport apron.

(C) At the airport.

第二十七題，請看這三張圖。第二十七題，注意聆聽接下來的廣播。你最有可能在哪裡聽到這則廣播？

各位先生女士，這是機長廣播。我們即將通過一些亂流。為了您的安全，請立即回到座位上並繫好您的安全帶。謝謝您的合作。

選項：(A) 飛機上。

(B) 停機坪。

(C) 機場。

答案 A

28. For question number 28, please look at the three pictures. Question number 28, listen to the following short talk. What will Lisa most probably do now?

Lisa has been working in front of the computer for more than four hours. She has got a stiff back and neck. She needs to do something to make her feel better so as to get back to work.

第二十八題，請看這三張圖。第二十八題，注意聆聽接下來的簡短談話。麗莎現在最有可能做什麼？

麗莎已經在電腦前工作超過四小時了。她背部和頸部僵硬。她需要做些事讓她覺得好一點才能繼續工作。

(A) Travel abroad.

(B) Go shopping.

(C) Stretch her body.

選項：(A) 出國旅行。

(B) 逛街。

(C) 做伸展操。

答案 C

29. For question number 29, please look at the three pictures. Question number 29, listen to the following short talk. What will Keri most likely have for lunch? Keri loves to bake, so she made some bread and cookies this morning. She is going to have lunch now. Although she has made bread and cookies, she wants to save them and have them later. Instead, she feels like having noodles now.

(A) Bread.

(B) Sushi.

(C) Noodles.

第二十九題，請看這三張圖。第二十九題，注意聆聽接下來的簡短談話。凱莉最有可能吃什麼當午餐？

凱莉熱愛烘焙，所以她今早做了些麵包和餅乾。她現在要吃午餐了。雖然她已經做了麵包和餅乾，但她想把它們留到等一下再吃。她現在想吃麵。

選項：(A) 麵包。

(B) 壽司。

(C) 麵。

答案 C

30. For question number 30, please look at the three pictures. Question number 30, Helen left a message on Cathy's answering machine. What will Cathy most probably do tomorrow?

Hi, Cathy. It's me, Helen. Kate and I will go on a picnic tomorrow. I wondered if you were free tomorrow. If you would like to come with us, please call me.

(A) Cook.

(B) Read.

(C) Go for a picnic.

第三十題，請看這三張圖。第三十題，海倫在凱西的答錄機裡留了言。凱西明天最有可能做什麼？

嗨，凱西，我是海倫。我和凱特明天要去野餐。不知道你明天有沒有空。如果你想要跟我們一起去的話，請打電話給我。

選項：(A) 煮東西。

(B) 閱讀。

(C) 野餐。

答案 C

第一部份：看圖辨義

1. For question number 1, please look at picture A. Question number 1:

   What is the woman going to do?

   (A) She's going to dance.

   (B) She's going to swim.

   (C) She's going to sleep.

   答案　**B**

   第一題，請看圖片 A。第一題：

   這女生將要做什麼？

   選項：(A) 她將要跳舞。

   　　　(B) 她將要游泳。

   　　　(C) 她將要睡覺。

2. For questions number 2 and 3, please look at picture B. Question number 2:

   What are they doing?

   (A) They're running.

   (B) They're dancing.

   (C) They're singing.

   答案　**B**

   第二題及第三題，請看圖片 B。第二題：

   他們正在做什麼？

   選項：(A) 他們正在跑步。

   　　　(B) 他們正在跳舞。

   　　　(C) 他們正在唱歌。

3. Question number 3, please look at picture B again. Where are these people?

   (A) In a classroom.

   (B) In a ballroom.

   (C) In a restroom.

   答案　**B**

   第三題，請再看一次圖片 B。這些人在什麼地方？

   選項：(A) 在教室裡。

   　　　(B) 在舞廳裡。

   　　　(C) 在洗手間。

4. For question number 4, please look at picture C. Question number 4:

   Which activity is allowed to do in Collin Square Park?

   (A) Taking pictures.

   (B) Riding bikes.

   (C) Living in a tent.

   答案　**A**

   第四題，請看圖片 C。第四題：

   哪項活動在柯林廣場公園是允許的？

   選項：(A) 拍照。

   　　　(B) 騎腳踏車。

   　　　(C) 露營。

5. For question number 5, please look at picture D. Question number 5:
What do you see in the picture?
(A) A woman with short hair.
(B) A woman with glasses.
(C) A woman with a scarf.

第五題，請看圖片 D。第五題：

你在這張圖中看到什麼？
選項：(A) 一個短髮的女生。
　　　(B) 一個戴眼鏡的女生。
　　　(C) 一個圍著圍巾的女生。

答案　**A**

第二部份：問答

6. Come join us for dinner.
(A) Sorry, I didn't mean it.
(B) What's up?
(C) OK. Thanks!

來跟我們一起吃晚餐吧。
選項：(A) 抱歉，我不是故意的。
　　　(B) 怎麼了？
　　　(C) 好。謝謝你！

答案　**C**

7. Would you like to have some more ice cream?
(A) OK, I'm leaving now.
(B) Yes, orange juice will be fine.
(C) That'd be great. Thanks.

你要多吃一點冰淇淋嗎？

選項：(A) 好，我現在要走了。
　　　(B) 好，柳橙汁不錯。
　　　(C) 好啊。謝謝你。

答案　**C**

8. Thanks for your help. Here's a little something for you.
(A) How's everything?
(B) I'm glad to see you again.
(C) Oh, you shouldn't have.

謝謝你的幫忙。這是一點小東西要送你的。
選項：(A) 一切都好嗎？
　　　(B) 很高興再見到你。
　　　(C) 噢，你不必這樣。

答案　**C**

9. Why did you leave early yesterday?
(A) Yes, I left home 8 years ago.
(B) Oh, I got some work to do.
(C) I was wearing a T-shirt.

你昨天為什麼提早離開？
選項：(A) 是的，我八年前離開家。
　　　(B) 喔，我有一些工作要做。
　　　(C) 我那時正穿著 T 恤。

答案　**B**

10. Excuse me. The steak is overcooked.

    (A) Thank you very much.

    (B) I'm sorry. I'll change that for you.

    (C) Well, I'll cook later.

答案 **B**

不好意思。這牛排煎得太老了。

選項：(A) 非常謝謝你。

      (B) 很抱歉。我幫您換。

      (C) 那麼，我等一下再煮。

11. Do you know why Paul is absent today?

    (A) I'm sorry. I won't do it again.

    (B) Yes. He has a cold.

    (C) Sure. See you tomorrow.

答案 **B**

你知道保羅今天為何沒來嗎？

選項：(A) 抱歉。我不會再犯了。

      (B) 知道。他感冒了。

      (C) 當然。明天見。

12. James, you must have lost at least 20 pounds.

    (A) Yes, I'm lost.

    (B) No, I will buy 20 pounds.

    (C) Yes. Isn't it wonderful?

答案 **C**

詹姆士，你一定減了至少有二十磅的體重。

選項：(A) 是的，我迷路了。

      (B) 不，我要買二十磅。

      (C) 沒錯。你不覺得很棒嗎？

13. Why don't we go to the movies and then have a cup of coffee?

    (A) I have a date later. How about tomorrow?

    (B) Don't be silly. Who told you that?

    (C) That's right. I'm going to move tomorrow.

答案 **A**

我們何不去看電影，然後喝杯咖啡？

選項：(A) 我等等有個約會，明天呢？

      (B) 別傻了。誰告訴你的？

      (C) 沒錯。我明天就要搬走了。

14. Which one is Susan?

    (A) I've known her since we were kids.

    (B) She is in my class.

    (C) She's the one in the white dress.

答案 **C**

哪一位是蘇珊？

選項：(A) 我從小時候就認識她了。

      (B) 她在我的班上。

      (C) 她是穿白色套裝的那一個。

15. Where were you last night?

    (A) Tomorrow night will be fine.

    (B) I stayed at home.

你昨天晚上在哪裡？

選項：(A) 明天晚上可以。

      (B) 我待在家裡。

(C) That was the last time I saw her.

(C) 那是我最後一次看到她。

第三部份：簡短對話

16. M: Do you want to go to the basketball game with me?

    W: Of course, I'd like to. When is the game?

    M: This coming Friday.

    W: Oh, no. My aunt is coming to visit us on Friday.

    Q: Why did the woman refuse the man?

       (A) Her aunt is coming.

       (B) She'll practice basketball.

       (C) She doesn't like the man.

男：你要跟我一起去看籃球賽嗎？

女：當然，我很樂意。比賽是什麼時候？

男：這個星期五。

女：噢，不行。我姑媽星期五要來拜訪我們。

問題：這女生為何拒絕這男生？

選項：(A) 她姑媽要來。

(B) 她要練習籃球。

(C) 她不喜歡這男生。

17. M: Let's order a pizza for lunch.

    W: No, thanks. I don't like pizza.

    M: What would you like to have, then?

    W: Well, I think I'll just have some salad.

    Q: What is the woman going to have for lunch?

       (A) Pizza.

       (B) Salad.

       (C) Nothing.

男：我們午餐叫披薩來吃吧。

女：不，謝了。我不喜歡披薩。

男：那你想要吃什麼？

女：嗯，我想我就吃一些沙拉好了。

問題：這女生午餐將要吃什麼？

選項：(A) 披薩。

(B) 沙拉。

(C) 什麼都不吃。

18. M: Thank you for the motorcycle. I had great fun.

    W: Sure. So where did you go?

    M: I took my girlfriend to the beach.

    Q: Why did the man thank the woman?

       (A) She made fun of him.

男：謝謝你的機車。我玩得很開心。

女：當然。那你去了什麼地方？

男：我帶我女朋友去海灘。

問題：這男生為何感謝這女生？

選項：(A) 她開他的玩笑。

(B) She lent him the motorcycle.

(C) She took him to the beach.

(B) 她借他機車。

(C) 她帶他去海灘。

19. W: Hi, Sam, did you bring the book?

M: Huh? What book are you talking about?

W: My book. You promised to return it to me.

M: Oh, I'm terribly sorry. I forgot.

Q: Why did the man apologize to the woman?

(A) He lost the book.

(B) He bought another book.

(C) He forgot to bring the book.

女：嗨，山姆，你把書帶來了嗎？

男：啊？你在說什麼書？

女：我的書。你答應要拿來還我。

男：噢，非常抱歉。我忘了。

問題：這男生為何向這女生道歉？

選項：(A) 他把書弄丟了。

(B) 他買了另一本書。

(C) 他忘了帶那本書。

20. M: What would you like for dessert?

W: What are the choices?

M: We have ice cream, banana cake, and apple pie.

W: I'll have ice cream, thanks.

Q: Who are the speakers?

(A) A policeman and a driver.

(B) A waiter and a customer.

(C) A teacher and a student.

男：你想要什麼甜點？

女：有什麼選擇？

男：我們有冰淇淋、香蕉蛋糕和蘋果派。

女：我要冰淇淋，謝謝。

問題：這些說話者是誰？

選項：(A) 一位警察和一位駕駛。

(B) 一位服務生和一位顧客。

(C) 一位老師和一位學生。

21. M: Look! There are so many people.

W: They're waiting to see the baseball star.

M: Really? Let's line up, too.

W: I can't. I have to go home and help my mom prepare the dinner.

Q: Why are there so many people?

男：你看！那裡有好多人。

女：他們正在等著見一位棒球明星。

男：真的嗎？我們也來排隊吧。

女：我不行。我必須回家幫忙我媽媽準備晚餐。

問題：為什麼那裡有很多人？

(A) They are lining up.

(B) They are going home.

(C) They are waiting for a star.

選項：(A) 他們在排隊。

　　　(B) 他們要回家。

　　　(C) 他們在等一位明星。

答案　C

22. W: How is your tooth?

　　M: Much better, thank you. Dr. Lin is really good.

　　W: He is always gentle and patient, isn't he?

　　M: Yes. I used to be scared of seeing a doctor, but I'm not afraid anymore.

　　Q: What are the speakers talking about?

　　　(A) A student.

　　　(B) A teacher.

　　　(C) A dentist.

女：你的牙齒還好嗎？

男：好多了，謝謝你。林醫生真的很棒。

女：他總是和善又有耐心，對不對？

男：是啊，我以前一直很害怕看醫生，但我不再害怕了。

問題：這些說話者在談論什麼？

選項：(A) 一位學生。

　　　(B) 一位老師。

　　　(C) 一位牙醫。

答案　C

23. W: Do you like my new apartment?

　　M: It's great. It's very close to the bus stop.

　　W: Yes. That's why I like it, too. But I think it's a little bit too small.

　　M: Well, I really don't care about that.

　　Q: Why do the speakers like this apartment?

　　　(A) It is small.

　　　(B) The rent is cheap.

　　　(C) It is near the bus stop.

女：你喜歡我的新公寓嗎？

男：很不錯。離公車站很近。

女：沒錯。那也是我喜歡它的原因。不過我覺得它有點太小了。

男：其實，我不太在意這個。

問題：為什麼這些說話者喜歡這間公寓？

選項：(A) 它很小。

　　　(B) 房租很便宜。

　　　(C) 離公車站很近。

答案　C

24. M: Well, how about this watch? It's only NT$1,900.

　　W: Oh, I like it very much, but it's too expensive for me.

男：那麼，這支手錶如何？只要新臺幣一千九百元。

女：噢，我是很喜歡，不過對我而言太貴了。

M: I see. Let me find another one for you.

Q: Where are these two people?

    (A) In a train station.

    (B) In a bookstore.

    (C) In a watch shop.

男：我了解。讓我再找另外一支給你。

問題：這兩人在什麼地方？

選項：(A) 在火車站裡。

    (B) 在書店裡。

    (C) 在鐘錶行裡。

答案　C

25. W: Tony, could you please answer this question?

M: I'm sorry, madam. I have no idea about it.

W: Well, maybe you should study harder from now on. Please come to my office after school.

Q: Why does the teacher ask Tony to go to her office?

    (A) He forgot to do his homework.

    (B) He didn't study for the exam.

    (C) He wasn't able to answer the question.

女：湯尼，請你回答這個問題好嗎？

男：老師，對不起。我不知道答案。

女：嗯，也許你從現在開始應該更用功一點。放學後，請到我的辦公室。

問題：為什麼這位老師要求湯尼到她的辦公室？

選項：(A) 他忘記寫作業。

    (B) 他沒有準備考試內容。

    (C) 他沒有辦法回答問題。

答案　C

第四部份：短文聽解

26. For question number 26, please look at the three pictures. Question number 26, listen to the following short talk. What will Jenny most probably take with her? It rained heavily this morning when Jenny left home for school. She didn't like to wear a raincoat, so she took her umbrella and went to school on foot instead of by bike.

第二十六題，請看這三張圖。第二十六題，注意聆聽接下來的簡短談話。珍妮最有可能帶著什麼？

今天早上當珍妮要去學校的時候雨下得很大。她不喜歡穿雨衣，所以她帶了雨傘走路去上學而不是騎腳踏車。

(A) An umbrella.

(B) A raincoat.

(C) A watch.

答案　**A**

27. For question number 27, please look at the three pictures. Question number 27, listen to the following short talk. What animal will the Lins most probably visit in the zoo?

Mr. and Mrs. Lin want to take their son to the zoo to see an animal. It's an Australian animal with no tail. It lives almost entirely on eucalyptus leaves and needs to sleep 16 to 18 hours a day.

(A) Kangaroo.

(B) Panda.

(C) Koala.

第二十七題，請看這三張圖。第二十七題，注意聆聽接下來的簡短談話。林家人最有可能到動物園裡看什麼動物？

林先生和林太太想帶他們的兒子到動物園看一種動物。牠是澳洲沒有尾巴的動物。牠幾乎以尤加利葉維生而且一天需要睡十六至十八個小時。

選項：(A) 袋鼠。

(B) 熊貓。

(C) 無尾熊。

答案　**C**

28. For question number 28, please look at the three pictures. Question number 28, Mr. Smith is leaving a phone message for his wife. Where will Mr. Smith most likely go?

Hey, it's me. I'm driving home from work. I will arrive home later than usual because my car is running out of gas. I'll have to fill up the tank before heading home.

(A) A parking lot.

(B) A coffee shop.

(C) A gas station.

第二十八題，請看這三張圖。第二十八題，史密斯先生正在留語音訊息給他的妻子。史密斯先生最有可能去哪裡？

嘿，是我。我正在開車從公司回家。我會比平常晚到家，因為我的車快沒汽油了。我必須在回家之前先把油箱加滿。

選項：(A) 停車場。

(B) 咖啡店。

(C) 加油站。

答案　**C**

29. For question number 29, please look at the three pictures. Question number 29, listen to the following message. What does Alice ask her mother to do?

Hello, Mom. I will be in Paris next week on business. Would you please swing by my house to feed my cat? I will pack my bags at home today. When you hear the message, call me! Bye.

(A) Clean the house.

(B) Pack bags.

(C) Feed the cat.

答案 **C**

第二十九題，請看這三張圖。第二十九題，注意聆聽接下來的留言。愛麗絲請她母親做什麼？

哈囉，媽。我下禮拜要到巴黎出差。你可以順道來我家幫我餵貓嗎？我今天會在家整理行李。當你聽到留言的時候再打給我！再見。

選項：(A) 打掃房子。

(B) 整理行李。

(C) 餵貓。

30. For question number 30, please look at the three pictures. Question number 30, listen to the following message. What will Kevin most probably do?

Hi, Mark, this is Kevin. I'm sorry, I can't play basketball with you this afternoon. My parents went to visit my grandparents this morning, and they won't be home till 9 o'clock. So, I have to take care of my little sister. So maybe next time. Bye.

(A) Read a book.

(B) Play basketball.

(C) Take care of his little sister.

答案 **C**

第三十題，請看這三張圖。第三十題，注意聆聽接下來的留言。凱文最有可能做什麼？

嗨，馬克，我是凱文。我很抱歉我今天下午無法跟你一起打籃球了。我的父母今早去拜訪我的祖父母，他們到九點前都不會回來。所以，我必須照顧我的妹妹。或許下一次吧，再見。

選項：(A) 看書。

(B) 打籃球。

(C) 照顧妹妹。

第一部份：看圖辨義

1. For questions number 1 and 2, please look at picture A. Question number 1: What is this invitation about?

   (A) A dinner party.

   (B) A birthday party.

   (C) A wedding.

   第一題及第二題，請看圖片 A。第一題：

   這張邀請函是關於什麼？

   選項：(A) 一場晚宴。

   (B) 一場生日派對。

   (C) 一場婚禮。

   答案 C

2. Question number 2, please look at picture A again. What time will the event begin?

   (A) At 5 p.m.

   (B) On Saturday afternoon.

   (C) On June 15.

   第二題，請再看一次圖片 A。這個活動將在幾點開始？

   選項：(A) 下午五點。

   (B) 星期六下午。

   (C) 六月十五日。

   答案 A

3. For question number 3, please look at picture B. Question number 3: When will John meet Mary?

   (A) Mary.

   (B) In the theater.

   (C) 7 p.m.

   第三題，請看圖片 B。第三題：

   約翰將在什麼時候跟瑪莉碰面？

   選項：(A) 瑪莉。

   (B) 在劇院裡。

   (C) 晚上七點。

   答案 C

4. For question number 4, please look at picture C. Question number 4: What is happening in the picture?

   (A) Tom is throwing a ball.

   (B) Jason is holding a baseball bat.

   (C) Sam is dancing on the field.

   第四題，請看圖片 C。第四題：

   圖片中發生了什麼事？

   選項：(A) 湯姆正在丟一顆球。

   (B) 傑森正在握著一支棒球棍。

   (C) 山姆正在球場上跳舞。

   答案 B

5. For question number 5, please look at picture D. Question number 5:

   第五題，請看圖片 D。第五題：

What is the man doing?

(A) He is listening to the music.

(B) He is cutting the steak.

(C) He is cooking dinner.

> 答案 **B**

這男生在做什麼？

選項：(A) 他正在聽音樂。

(B) 他正在切牛排。

(C) 他正在煮晚餐。

第二部份：問答

6. Do you want to go hiking with me?

(A) The game is over.

(B) Sure. That would be fun.

(C) Yes, enjoy your food.

> 答案 **B**

你要跟我去健行嗎？

選項：(A) 遊戲結束了。

(B) 好啊。那應該很有趣。

(C) 是的，請慢用。

7. Don't you want some more rice?

(A) Yes, I don't.

(B) No, I'd like more.

(C) No, thanks. I'm full.

> 答案 **C**

你不想要再來一些白飯嗎？

選項：(A) 是的，我不要。

(B) 不，我想要多一點。

(C) 不，謝了。我吃飽了。

8. Thank you for what you did for me.

(A) I'm sorry.

(B) It was nothing.

(C) We're late.

> 答案 **B**

謝謝你為我做的事。

選項：(A) 我很抱歉。

(B) 那沒什麼。

(C) 我們遲到了。

9. I'm sorry I broke your cup. Please forgive me.

(A) You are welcome.

(B) Thank you.

(C) That's OK.

> 答案 **C**

很抱歉我打破了你的杯子。請原諒我。

選項：(A) 不客氣。

(B) 謝謝你。

(C) 沒關係。

10. Can you stop the music? It's too loud.

(A) Really? I hate music.

(B) How do you like the food?

(C) I'm really sorry about that.

你可以把音樂關掉嗎？太吵了。

選項：(A) 真的嗎？我討厭音樂。

(B) 你覺得這食物如何？

(C) 真是對不起。

11. What do you like to do in your free time?

    (A) I'm not free tonight.

    (B) I'm going home now.

    (C) I like to exercise.

你空閒時候喜歡做什麼？

選項：(A) 我今晚沒空。

        (B) 我現在要回家了。

        (C) 我喜歡運動。

答案 **C**

12. I didn't know you were such a great dancer.

    (A) I don't know you, either.

    (B) Oh, thank you!

    (C) Let me show you how to write.

我不知道你是一個這麼棒的舞者。

選項：(A) 我也不認識你。

        (B) 噢，謝謝你！

        (C) 讓我為你示範如何寫作。

答案 **B**

13. How was your trip to Japan?

    (A) I don't like Chinese food.

    (B) I really had a great time.

    (C) Japan is close to Taiwan.

你的日本之旅如何？

選項：(A) 我不喜歡中式料理。

        (B) 我真的玩得很開心。

        (C) 日本離臺灣很近。

答案 **B**

14. Who's that tall guy over there?

    (A) Yes. It is my dog.

    (B) He is my brother.

    (C) They are my classmates.

那邊那位高個子是誰？

選項：(A) 是的，牠是我的狗。

        (B) 他是我兄弟。

        (C) 他們是我同學。

答案 **B**

15. How would you like your steak?

    (A) Coffee, please.

    (B) Medium, please.

    (C) Yes, please.

你想要你的牛排幾分熟？

選項：(A) 請給我咖啡。

        (B) 請給我五分熟。

        (C) 是的，麻煩你。

答案 **B**

第三部份：簡短對話

16. M: Do you want to go fishing?

    W: Well, I'm not crazy about fishing.

男：你想要去釣魚嗎？

女：嗯，我對釣魚沒那麼大興趣。看

How about a movie? | 電影如何？

M: OK. Let's go to a movie. | 男：沒問題。我們去看電影。

W: That'd be great. | 女：太好了。

Q: What will the man and woman do? | 問題：這男生和女生將要做什麼？

   (A) They will go fishing. | 選項：(A) 他們將會去釣魚。

   (B) They will go to a movie. | (B) 他們將會去看電影。

   (C) They will go shopping. | (C) 他們將會去購物。

答案 **B**

17. W: Would you like to have French fries? | 女：你要吃炸薯條嗎？

M: Well, I think I'll have a hamburger. | 男：喔，我想要一個漢堡。

W: Would you like to have a coke to go with it? | 女：要來杯可樂搭配嗎？

M: That'd be great. Thanks. | 男：這樣很好。謝了。

Q: What is the man going to have? | 問題：這男生將會吃什麼？

   (A) A hamburger and a coke. | 選項：(A) 漢堡和可樂。

   (B) French fries and a coke. | (B) 炸薯條和可樂。

   (C) A hamburger and French fries. | (C) 漢堡和炸薯條。

答案 **A**

18. M: I'd like to invite you to dinner. | 男：我想邀請你吃晚餐。

W: Why? What did I do? | 女：為什麼？我做了什麼嗎？

M: You helped me with my paper. Remember? | 男：你幫助我完成了作業的報告。記得嗎？

W: Oh, I remember it. So, did you pass the course? | 女：噢，我想起來了。那麼，你那門課有及格嗎？

Q: What did the woman do for the man? | 問題：這女生為這男生做了什麼？

   (A) She took him to dinner. | 選項：(A) 她帶他去吃晚餐。

   (B) She helped him with his paper. | (B) 她幫助他完成作業。

   (C) She gave him a high score. | (C) 她給他一個很高的分數。

答案 **B**

19. W: Jack, can you turn the TV down? | 女：傑克，你可以把電視轉小聲嗎？

M: Sure, but why? | 男：當然可以，但為什麼要轉小聲？

W: I'm on the phone.

M: Oops. I'm sorry.

Q: What would Jack do next?

    (A) Talk on the phone.

    (B) Turn down the volume.

    (C) Turn on the TV.

女：我正在講電話。

男：噢。我很抱歉。

問題：傑克接下來會做什麼？

選項：(A) 講電話。

      (B) 把音量調低。

      (C) 把電視打開。

答案 B

20. W: Tracy and Karen are not here yet.

M: What? There are only 10 minutes left.

W: I know. The train is coming.

M: Maybe we should call them now.

Q: Where are the speakers?

    (A) At the airport.

    (B) At the train station.

    (C) At the bus station.

女：崔西和凱倫還沒到。

男：什麼？只剩下十分鐘了。

女：我知道。火車就快要來了。

男：也許我們應該立刻打給他們。

問題：說話者在什麼地方？

選項：(A) 在機場。

      (B) 在火車站。

      (C) 在公車站。

答案 B

21. M: Barbara, you didn't do well in the test this time. Are you OK?

W: Oh, Mr. Morgan, I'm sorry. I just spent too much time online. I'll study harder.

M: OK. Keep your word. I'll see if you do a better job next time.

Q: Who is this man?

    (A) Barbara's brother.

    (B) Barbara's boyfriend.

    (C) Barbara's teacher.

男：芭芭拉，這次你考試考得不好。你還好嗎？

女：噢，摩根老師，我很抱歉。我只是花太多時間上網了。我會更用功讀書。

男：好，要說話算話。我會看你下次是否表現得更好。

問題：這男生是誰？

選項：(A) 芭芭拉的兄弟。

      (B) 芭芭拉的男朋友。

      (C) 芭芭拉的老師。

答案 C

22. M: The weather report said it's going to rain this afternoon.

W: But it's sunny outside. I don't think it will rain.

男：氣象報告說今天下午會下雨。

女：不過現在外面陽光普照。我不認為會下雨。

M: You'd better take an umbrella just in case.

Q: What are they talking about?

   (A) Weather.

   (B) Clothes.

   (C) Umbrella.

男：你最好還是帶著雨傘以防萬一。

問題：他們在談論什麼？

選項：(A) 天氣。

      (B) 衣著。

      (C) 雨傘。

答案 **A**

23. M: I'm going to the supermarket to buy some carrots. Do you want me to buy anything for you?

W: Oh, bring me some fruit, please.

M: Sure, I will. Do you need some eggs?

W: No, thanks. There are still several eggs in the refrigerator.

Q: What might the man buy for the woman?

   (A) Eggs.

   (B) Apples.

   (C) Carrots.

男：我要去超級市場買些胡蘿蔔。你要我幫你買些東西嗎？

女：噢，請幫我帶些水果。

男：沒問題，我會的。你需要一些蛋嗎？

女：不用，謝謝。冰箱裡還有幾顆蛋。

問題：這男生可能會幫這女生買什麼？

選項：(A) 蛋。

      (B) 蘋果。

      (C) 胡蘿蔔。

答案 **B**

24. M: Where are we going to eat dinner? I'm so hungry.

W: I don't know. Any ideas?

M: I know a French restaurant just around the corner. The food there tastes really good.

W: Really? But I don't have enough money.

M: Don't worry. It's my treat.

Q: What is the man going to do?

   (A) Cook French food for the woman.

男：我們要去哪裡吃晚餐呢？我肚子好餓。

女：我不知道。有任何想法嗎？

男：我知道一間在附近的法式餐廳。那裡的食物真的很美味。

女：真的嗎？但是我的錢不夠。

男：別擔心，我請客。

問題：這男生將要做什麼？

選項：(A) 為這女生烹飪法式料理。

(B) Buy the woman dinner.

(C) Lend the woman some money.

答案 **B**

25. M: May I help you, madam?

W: I don't know what to order.

M: You should try our steak. It's very delicious.

W: Sounds good.

Q: Who was the man?

(A) A driver.

(B) A writer.

(C) A waiter.

答案 **C**

第四部份：短文聽解

26. For question number 26, please look at the three pictures. Question number 26, listen to the following short talk. What is Amy's favorite animal?

Amy is an animal lover. She keeps a dog and a rabbit in her apartment. She also wants to have a cat because she likes cats most.

(A) Rabbit.

(B) Cat.

(C) Dog.

答案 **B**

27. For question number 27, please look at the three pictures. Question number 27, listen to the following short talk. Why was Harold grounded by his parents?

Harold has been depressed lately. He

(B) 請這女生吃晚餐。

(C) 借給這女生一些錢。

男：女士，有什麼我可以幫忙的嗎？

女：我不知道該點什麼。

男：你應該試試看我們的牛排。它非常美味。

女：聽起來不錯。

問題：這男生是誰？

選項：(A) 一位司機。

(B) 一位作家。

(C) 一位服務生。

第二十六題，請看這三張圖。第二十六題，注意聆聽接下來的簡短對談。愛咪最喜愛的動物是什麼？

愛咪是個愛動物的人。她在她的公寓裡養了一隻狗和一隻兔子。她也想養一隻貓因為她最喜歡的是貓。

選項：(A) 兔子。

(B) 貓。

(C) 狗。

第二十七題，請看這三張圖。第二十七題，注意聆聽接下來的簡短對談。哈勒德為什麼被他父母禁足？

哈勒德最近很憂鬱。他花了大多數的

spent most of his time on outdoor activities. What's worse, he failed the exam. His parents were very angry about that. Therefore, he was grounded.

(A) He played video games.

(B) He failed the exam.

(C) He was late for school.

28. For question number 28, please look at the three pictures. Question number 28, listen to the following message for Betty. What did Betty order in the department store?

Hi, Betty. This is Olivia from San Min Department Store. The T-shirt you ordered has just arrived, so you can come to take it. By the way, a sky-blue skirt just arrived. I think it is a perfect match for your T-shirt and maybe you can try it on.

(A) A pair of pants.

(B) A pair of shoes.

(C) A T-shirt.

29. For question number 29, please look at the three pictures. Question number 29, listen to the following short talk. Which way will Ted most probably choose?

Ted is ordering a book from an overseas publisher. And he wants to have it as soon as possible. The publisher can deliver the book to him by sea, which

時間在戶外活動上。更糟的是,他考試不及格。他的父母對此很生氣。所以,他被禁足了。

選項:(A) 打電動。

(B) 考試不及格。

(C) 上學遲到。

第二十八題,請看這三張圖。第二十八題,注意聆聽接下來給貝蒂的留言。貝蒂在這家百貨公司訂了什麼?

嗨,貝蒂。我是三民百貨公司的奧莉薇雅。你訂的 T 恤剛剛到了,你可以來拿它。對了,有一件天藍色的裙子剛到。我認為它很適合搭你的 T 恤,或許你可以試穿看看。

選項:(A) 褲子。

(B) 鞋子。

(C) T 恤。

第二十九題,請看這三張圖。第二十九題,注意聆聽接下來的簡短對談。泰德最有可能會選擇哪一種運輸方式?

泰德在一家海外的出版社訂了一本書。而且他想要快點得到它。出版社可以藉由海運把書送給他,這樣一來書會在一個月內抵達,或是藉由空運,

will arrive in a month, or by air, which will arrive in five days.

(A) By air.

(B) By rail.

(C) By sea.

書就會在五天內抵達。

選項：(A) 空運。

     (B) 陸運。

     (C) 海運。

答案 **A**

30. For question number 30, please look at the three pictures. Question number 30, listen to the following announcement. What is the lost boy most likely wear? Attention please! A little boy wearing a gray T-shirt, blue jeans and a yellow cap has been found in the store. Anyone missing a child please contact the front desk immediately. Thank you.

(A) A skirt.

(B) A suit and tie.

(C) A T-shirt, jeans and a cap.

第三十題，請看這三張圖。第三十題，注意聆聽接下來的廣播。走失的男孩最有可能穿什麼？

請注意！我們在店內發現一位身穿灰色 T 恤，藍色牛仔褲和黃色帽子的小男孩。有小孩走失的人請馬上與櫃檯聯絡。謝謝。

選項：(A) 裙子。

     (B) 穿西裝打領帶。

     (C) 一件 T 恤、牛仔褲、和帽子。

答案 **C**

輕鬆讀出國中必備字彙力
Build Vocabulary through Reading

Susan M. Swier　編著

**首創四段式單字記憶法，
讓你輕鬆讀出字彙力！**

★ STEP 1 聲音：先看單字表，搭配三民東大學習網線上音檔，跟著音檔將單
字大聲唸出來，記住正確發音及拼字。

★ STEP 2 圖像：仔細看圖，搭配單字表找找看圖中隱含的單字。情境式圖像
會激發右腦學習，直接加深對字義的印象。

★ STEP 3 情境：閱讀故事，透過上下文來理解單字含意並掌握道地用法，比
看例句更有效！故事的情境將促使建立單字的長期記憶。

★ STEP 4 應用：透過每課練習題實際應用單字，驗收學習成效並加強記憶。
練習題含仿會考單題，同時提升會考戰力。隨書另附 15 回
隨堂評量。

哈佛英聽講堂

曾郁淇 著

什麼神奇的動作可以1分鐘化解緊張情緒？

英文簡報或辯論，如何一出場就有氣勢？

申請國內外大學，致勝關鍵到底是什麼？

世界各地自由行，怎麼樣跟任何人都能聊？

★ 60回家庭、校園、社交生活情境對話，全面擴增英聽背景知識。

★ 300題英語聽力測驗試題，完整備戰各類英聽測驗。

★ 全書特聘專業外籍錄音原錄製對話音檔，輕鬆聽、跟著說，聽說英
  文原來這麼簡單！

本書可搭配108課綱的加深加廣選修課程
「英語聽講」，讓你無縫接軌新課綱！

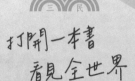

全民英檢新制上路，應試SO EASY！

◆ 完全符合新制全民英檢初級聽力測驗，讓你掌握最新題型。

◆ 全書共12回，情境、用字、語法等皆符合全民英檢初級程度。

◆ 提供試題範例分析，精闢解說各題型解題技巧與出題方向。

◆ 解析採用活動式的夾冊設計，讓你輕鬆對照題目，方便閱讀。

◆ 隨書附電子朗讀音檔，由專業外籍錄音員錄製。讓你培養語感、提升應試熟悉度。

三民網路書店
www.sanmin.com.tw

題本與解答本不分售
03-80707G